DAYDREAMERS

DAYDREAMERS

ALVIN LU

TUSCALOOSA

FC2 is an imprint of the University of Alabama Press

Inquiries about reproducing material from this work should be addressed to the University of Alabama Press

Book Design: Publications Unit, Department of English, Illinois State University; Director: Steve Halle, Production Assistant: Greta Terfruchte
Cover design: Matthew Revert, based on a concept by Steve Barbaro
Typeface: Adobe Caslon Pro (text) and Avenir (titles)

Library of Congress Cataloging-in-Publication Data is available from the Library of Congress.

ISBN: 978-1-57366-212-3
E-ISBN: 978-1-57366-915-3

What follows is a translation of a manuscript found among my father's papers. The translation is mine. Undertaking this task, and demurring from the same for the actually published work, is a personal decision, in that I am neither a writer nor translator by trade and the nature of the manuscript's connection to me, aside from it having been written by my father, is apparent from its very beginning.

One can say all one has to go on is on the page, which very well may put the identity of the author in question, even though the handwriting, delimited by squares printed on tissue-thin leaves of Chinese writing paper, running in vertical columns arranged in right-to-left sequence, bears a superficial resemblance to my father's. Clearly the manuscript differs in genre from the books he published in his lifetime: a memoir about raising a musical prodigy (my sister, not myself) and a pair of collections of desultory sǎnwén about his childhood and later adult life in the California suburbs, articles he had placed in Taiwanese newspapers over the years. These were works of nonfiction, of an autobiographical nature, even if in them he comes across as a distant observer of himself, much as he did in person. The manuscript, on the other hand, bears novelistic traces, even as it is preoccupied with the truth. What lends it this quality, as will become obvious, is the choice of protagonist, who I know, insofar as I know myself, is not the author, but someone whose mind he presumes to speak for. I suppose it is that way with all Chinese fathers and their sons.

Although he enjoyed a moment of fame in the insular world he portrayed with some degree of fidelity, he always thought of himself as an amateur, in that unbroken line of literati dabblers of the classical tradition. Because of language and cultural barriers, I had no reason to pay heed to this self-flattering persona—he was always my father, a civil engineer at a federal research laboratory—but that conception of himself occurred to me when I considered the other remarkable aspect of the manuscript, that is to say, its lack of polish. It was not something meant for publication, I thought, or if it was, it was still drafts away from its aim. Evidence of this unfinished state are the borrowed texts interwoven throughout, especially those taken from Yvonne Fung. It is unclear if these were meant for the manuscript as is, which would require permission for use, or were to be later slyly blended in, after having been reworked in the author's own voice, their provenance disguised. As they are, the excerpts consist of pages literally torn from Fung's published works and Scotch taped to the paper. In some cases, my father's own writing is scrawled around these sections. I have translated them in good faith, there being no official English versions of Fung's works available, and set them off with crude font changes, an effect that may come across as clumsy, but in this case I believe emulates my father's original labors. One can only speculate why he would include passages from another, more celebrated author's writing, someone whom he knew personally, and who plays a significant role in this narrative. Envy comes to mind. He never hinted as much to me, or at much emotion at all, but it underlies the oblique accusations of plagiarism that surface later in the story.

Two other sources of borrowed texts that appear, which I have also translated and indicated by formatting, are selections by himself, from the book about my sister and an unattributed fragment. Regarding the former, they are treated in the same manner as the excerpts from Fung's, clipped and taped from a printed edition. For background about the latter, see my footnote at the end of its appearance.

On the timing of the composition, I have nothing to go on besides the chronology of the narrative itself. He never spoke to us of his literary efforts, "us" meaning myself and my sister. Even when I was a child at home, when he would have been working on the articles that became his memoir, I never caught him in the act, so to speak. It is a mystery when he did write, although I imagine it must have been late, after we had all gone to bed. This manuscript, the last he ever worked on, based on the evidence, was of course put together following the events it relates, many of which can be corroborated by my own memory. The physical fact of the insertion of fragments from Fung's sole "nonfiction novel" places it after the event of that publication, which the manuscript also narrates. From there, though, is a road of many long years. How far back did he recall, if what he set down can be called recollections? Given some of those scenes, rendered in striking detail, scenes which have begun to recede into mere tremblings of feeling in my own memory, it seems it would not have been long after their occurrence, when they would have still been fresh in his mind. On the other hand, he possessed a keen memory, one honed, no doubt, by his day job. To the end, he had a superior mental ability to all of us, certainly to mine and maybe even to my sister's. It would not have surprised me if the composition had come much later in his career.

But it was not only a matter of recordkeeping. The genre he chose lent itself to delusion. The flaw of the manuscript, if I may venture an opinion, comes near the end, where we are asked to believe that the character in question, the antagonist, has infiltrated the imaginations of both authors, decades apart in time. I do not doubt that she ended up as my father's idée fixe. That she was a real person, upon whom others, including Yvonne Fung, projected their theories, is certain. But it was my father's conceit to suggest forces at work greater than the minds of creative writers turning upon a theme. I leave the reader to her own devices, but it strikes me that Fung could very well have been lying about having never read my father's memoir, or that she had, or heard about it, forgotten about it, and then unconsciously resurrected its ending.

As for whether or not, from my point of view, what happened happened, I can attest that my father, quite remarkably, got most of it right. I have spoken of the quality of his mind, glimmering in outline behind the account Fung claimed never to have read, so it does not surprise me that he could have watched his son's actions from afar and, with fiction's sleight of hand, conjured a passable version of not only those actions,

but what was going through the head of the character performing them. Sometimes he got it wrong, when, exactly, I will
not comment. Other times, as in the scene where I finally met
up with Lena Wu, I think he knew he was not just wrong,
but embellishing for the sake of formal balance, which was his
perpetual obligation. I can say, though, in real life that meeting
never occurred. As far as I am concerned, the ghost we were
chasing was simply that, a specter haunting my father's dreams.
It tormented him enough that he felt compelled to exorcise it
by writing this book.

{1}

WHEN MY FATHER SENT ME ON THAT ERRAND, it occurred to me, as I walked up the driveway to Ms. Hu's, that one way or another they had made it, their own literature, with their own books. It was a circumscribed literature, to be sure, with an audience solely of its authors, but for that not devoid of interest and, in spite of it all, published. If they were not household names—in this day and age where the meaning of a household was a slippery one, never mind ones whose halls did not ring with the names of authors—it was because their books were printed in a deprecated language and format: vertical columns, running right to left, in characters read by steadily dwindling numbers around the world. Such were their circumstances, it was their tradition to lament, even as their education had inculcated in them a notion of the literary that existed by definition outside the merely circumstantial. In this unprepossessing location, among what locals referred to as the outer avenues, the swirling sea fog choked truncated driveways and square, dying lawns. Behind the veil was to be found, if one only knew the right address, the last outpost of a civilization.

I had passed row after row of colorful two-story homes, each a uniform stack of single-floor living area set on top of a garage, and each two-story stack set horizontally against one another, so that collectively they formed neat rows along streets that had numbers for names. These north-south rows, in turn, were crossed by long boulevards that ran to the ocean, where the marine effects grew thicker. The result was two multicolored grids, one laying on top of the other, and the monotony of them was only occasionally interrupted by the appearance of a church, Chinese restaurant, or streetcar scraping through a turn at an intersection, before entering the fog.

There was a waist-high chain-link fence with a gate that could be opened by a latch, and beyond that, a discontinuous concrete walkway dividing a yellowing lawn. I rang the doorbell at a metal gate and was buzzed into a secondary exterior, a narrow, almost Moorish patio, with nothing in the wasted marking off of space but trash bins, a door to what presumably was the garage, and stairs to the second-floor entrance.

Twine handles dug into my fingers, which held the paper bag, from which protruded the ends of a pair of scrolls. If you were to unscroll them, you would find landscapes in the classical style, that is, guóhuà (literally, nation + painting), seaside scenes, cliffs and waves, and birds. What lent the bag weight, though, were not the paintings, but the books. I had examined them before coming here, six altogether, printed in the aforementioned format. Three of them would not mean anything to most people, but two might to a certain kind of reader. The one about an oedipal struggle set in Taipei had garnered notoriety in its day for its impenetrability, while the other was written by someone who counted as a local literary celebrity. She was an acquaintance of my parents, if not a close friend, having, as I recalled, attended some of their dinner parties. Checking the photo on the gatefold flap, I found a young woman in browline glasses, wearing what looked to be a school-uniform blouse. It had been taken a long time ago.

The third book was *the book*, my father's. It was his most well known out of the three that were published during the brief time he felt compelled to do such things, at an age when he should have been over it, and it had been well-known enough to serve as his entrée into . . . well, just what was this, exactly?

Ms. Hu was sitting at a table in a blue kimono jacket and white socks, and but for the more or less modern clothes, giving off the air of someone not of our world and time. There was some clutter, but no sign of someone who had lost her mind. Two horizontal, panoramic landscapes occupied the main room, a living area that had been adapted into a kind of studio. One hung framed on the longest wall, where most people would have put a flat-screen TV. The other, on a perpendicular plane, lay half finished on a worktable in the middle of the room. Floor-to-ceiling slat windows faced the street, but with the shades pulled. What seemed like clutter, stacked sheets of paper and organized brushes and inks, had been placed within reach for the small woman who could not move very well.

After the opening courtesies, I got to the point.

"I'm here to return these."

I placed the bag at her feet. She ignored it. Instead of what I came to discuss, she wanted to hear my opinion on the "verdict." It was not something I had given much thought to, although it had been all the talk in her and my parents' circle.

"The 'killer' . . . " she spoke hoarsely, "I suppose he was acquitted . . . but then again, he *did* kill somebody, didn't he?"

There had been an untimely death among us; the scandal behind it had shocked the whole community. That latter is a term I hesitate to use, but given how the reaction reverberated, in the collective and seemingly the same way with all its members, this seemed an instance where that lazy shorthand proved justified. For all their years in America, my parents' *community* did not think the wall between their almost-secret daily lives and the news was so thin, but this case, involving a successful businessman, someone who would have been deemed a scholar in another time, that is to say, one of their own, being faulted with his own murder, tore away the illusion that their lives could not be spoken about by others. According to the evidence, Rafael, or "Uncle Rafael," as I had known him, had somehow gotten ahold of the weapon that was eventually turned against him. Talk about blaming the victim! He was there, gun in hand, to shoot his lover's lover. Everyone was sure he didn't mean to go through with it. He had just wanted to put a scare into the younger man. If he had succeeded in what he had been accused of, he would probably be in jail now. That seemed an even crazier outcome, but Uncle Rafael would still be alive then, and he would have just bore it out as his fate. The rest of us would stew over the injustice of it. These, however, were abstract scenarios.

"The man who killed him. He's a foreigner, isn't he? I mean, a real foreigner, from outside the country. He left as soon as his name was cleared. Is that true?"

"Seems that way."

"And the girl? Did she leave the country too?"

"Nobody knows where she is. But probably not." Everyone was so concerned about that couple, my father had complained. What about the dead? Would *his* name ever be cleared?

"Losing your life over a woman who's not even your wife seems like such a waste."

"My father still doesn't believe it."

"Yes, it was a business deal gone awry, not a lovers' triangle, that's what he told me. Your father's very loyal to his friends, but it doesn't look good for Rafael, does it? Not that he would care, where he is now." She reached into the bag, which she suddenly acknowledged the existence of. "If your father wants to clear Rafael Hsu's name, he should talk to Yvonne Fung. She's writing a story about this whole mess for a magazine." She pulled out the book with the photo of the young woman. "This is her best work. It's about the Cultural Revolution, which she experienced firsthand. As a writer, she knew enough by then to get out of the way of her material. Her earlier work, as you may know, was stylistically overburdened. Well, she's a realtor in Millbrae now. I offered her the chair to the Society, but she refused."

"So my father wasn't your first choice?" I didn't ask, out of courtesy, if he had a say in the matter.

"She's more famous. And she's an active writer. But your father's book is better. It's too bad he didn't write more."

"He always said he only did it because his friend asked him to."

"Yes, a simple memoir about bringing up your daughter. Not a grandiose topic like the Cultural Revolution. 'It was written in installments for a newspaper. It should never have been a book.' He told me that too. But your father didn't have to learn to get out of the way of his material, did he? He's that rare person who's naturally modest."

"It's probably why he never wrote anything else after that."

"They say it should come of its own, once you have something to say. But sometimes it's better to have nothing to say at all. Did your sister read it?"

"No. She can't read Chinese."

"Might be painful if she did. You should translate it."

No, I would rather not, I thought. What was it like raising a genius? That was the kind of topic the readers of the weekend supplement my father wrote for would be interested in. My sister did not turn out to be a genius, though, at least in the estimation of whoever decided such things. My father, in the way he came off in his writing, had been objective about it. He did not want to portray himself as that kind of parent, and maybe that was the source of the book's appeal.

"I'm too old to be doing this," she said. "Your father has to do it. There's no one left."

In here, where no doubt she wanted to stay, the twisty columns on the pages in those books mirrored what lay outside, a map. Those streets could be the tropical alleys of Taipei, only half lit at night, populated by extravagant, seed-spitting flowers, navigated by fathers out for twilight walks, never to return. They could have been Shanghai, as it used to be, in her memory of its zenith, and, later, that of Yvonne Fung's, in its days of political paranoia.

I made one last-ditch effort to leave the bag. Instead she took my hand and pressed my fingers around its handles. With a surprisingly strong grip, she led me to the door.

{2}

I HAD SOME GLIMMERING RECOLLECTION that this must once have been a very remote place, not so different from the location of its sister laboratory in the canyons of New Mexico. Nowadays there were still enough gaps in the sprawl chewing through the countryside that one could be tricked into thinking things were still what they were—turkey buzzards flocking over roadkill, horses galloping behind fences against a backdrop of vineyards and tawny hills—but this bucolic mirage occurred only if one had not been paying attention, which, given the mind-numbing effects of traffic, was likely.

The visitation from the past passed, and the house-barnacled hills swam back into view, followed by the appearance of electrified fences and walls topped by concertina wire. Tennis courts, an Olympic swimming pool, and a rubberized running track encroached upon a stranded oak tree; beyond it lay the greater expanse of a gated parking lot. "Pods" dotted the lower foothills in no apparent pattern, as if they had been dropped from a truck: structures that were the very manifestation of the provisional, although they had been there as long as I remember. My father had spent his entire career in them.

He had worked with some of the best minds on earth. Their jobs involved projects bigger than houses. I had a childhood memory of the slow construction of a fusion plant outside his office window, of giant magnets in a freshly dug pit, and a radiation suit, with a person inside it, waddling through the halls of the flimsy-looking Plutonium Center, its short, pale buildings not so different-looking than those of my junior high school. (Another memory was winning second prize, a Hewlett-Packard engineering calculator, in a laboratory-sponsored essay contest on the benefits of nuclear power.)

For those years, he did not have much else to show us, since he could not speak about his work for reasons of national security. As an adult now, I realize he had been withholding his heroism from us, the valor displayed in internecine battles, which on the surface, if they were ever known to the world at large, would seem petty, but which would have radical repercussions there. It seems hard to imagine now, since so much of our focus has turned toward the trivial, but they had been molding the stuff of reality. Now he was packing away his life's ambitions and setting them aside, going back to that world-at-large, in an exchange he never wanted. And yet, despite his achievements, he once wrote in one of his newspaper articles that the most impressed he had ever been by any technology was the time my uncle showed him the first video game he had ever seen. It was in a pizza parlor in Cupertino, and the reason he was so impressed was because of the reaction it got from my sister and me. Nothing he worked on could elicit such a response from us.

The inside of his office looked taller than it did from out-side. The high-ceilinged rooms, like the interior of a silo, did something to the air circulation, so it was ungodly stuffy, even with the HVAC turned on. One would think engineers would figure this stuff out. Sunlight fell across his desk; he was not here, but outside. I could see him through the window, running on the track, part of his daily prelunch routine, which he kept to, even on this last day. I turned the blinds. Everything in the room was stacked vertically, the laser printer resting on a shelf set on top of a monitor. I remember when the printer was a dot matrix, and the paper would accordion onto my head as it rolled out. Everything in the room seemed designed to fall on top of you. During one earthquake, the aluminum bookshelf, which was not fixed to a wall, did, almost killing him, the person responsible for structural stability. It was all still there, in suspense, ready to fall again. He had not started packing.

I stole a few plastic bins from the mail room and cleared his bookshelf, placing the fattest books first into the bins. It occurred to me that the laboratory might not want them taken out, since they, or the knowledge bound up in them, seemed important, but to whom would they have been worth bequeathing? The truth was that the road taken by my father, of a quiet life of government-funded research, was no longer what it once was. Was there anyone to take his place? The age of building new plants was past. Conversely, would my father have any use for these? Would anything he would ever do from now on require them? Probably not.

I told him I had gone to Ms. Hu's as he asked.

"What'd she say?"

"She wouldn't take the bag back."

He looked more annoyed than I thought he would be.

"So you still have it?"

"I brought it. It's in the car right now."

We carried the mail bins full of books and office supplies to the parking lot. On the drive in, the sky had been slate gray, but the clouds had grown darker, and the wind, which had been soft and temperate, hinted at something menacing. This valley served as a funnel for the dry breezes that blew across the Diablo Range, fueling the grass fires of autumn and, in calmer moments, powering the wind turbines that rose from the hills of Altamont Pass like robot redwoods.

"She said this is exactly the kind of thing you'll have more time for from now on."

"I don't have more time. I have less. As soon as I check out of here, I might have to make a trip to LA over this terrible business with Rafael. Ms. Hu should keep doing it. Her mind's sound, she's in great health."

The "terrible business," my mother told me, had left Uncle Rafael's widow looking to sell the company she now found herself solely in charge of. The reason he was going to LA was to offer his help, whether at her bequest or his own insistence, it was not clear. I reminded myself, too, that his real motive might be to hunt down the woman behind the whole scandal. Ms. Hu had thought he would try something like that, as part of his effort to restore Rafael's good name. What would he want from her, I wondered, even if he managed to track her down? To have her come clean, by admitting that she put Uncle Rafael up to it and was thus indirectly responsible for his death? To speak the truth of their relationship, in all its ugliness, not one of lovers, as everyone believed, but of business accomplices whose deal had gone south, as he suspected? Or was his intent, and I could imagine him very much wanting to do this, simply to subject her to his intolerable Confucian scolding? She might have escaped the law, but it would be more important that shame ring in her ears forever.

"She wants you to get in touch with a writer named Yvonne Fung. You know her, right? She's working on an article about Uncle Rafael."

"I do know her."

I imagined he did not want her interfering with whatever he had in mind. But just what did he have in mind? That was something I was never privy to, which made the experience of reading his writings, once the language became available to me, all the stranger. He had kept so much from us, none of it in terms of content particularly shocking, but the quality of his expression was something I had not expected.

"If you're heading down there anyway, I imagine she might want to go with you."

Surprisingly, he acquiesced to contacting her, even mentioning that having her accompany him might bring her around to his way of thinking. He sounded unusually hopeful. If they came across any evidence, as he imagined it, her article might be the start of a shift in public opinion about Rafael, such as it was.

In the car, an oscillating whine I mistook for engine noise played over the stereo: bursts of light between long stretches of darkness, gentle rocking back and forth between frequencies, dissonant cries bubbling up as if from inside a well, more alien than any impressionism I was familiar with. My sister was the one playing, the instrument she had played from childhood unrecognizable. She sent these to him instead of letters. She did not play this kind of thing in his book. In it, she was a young girl studying the usual repertory, with an entire chapter devoted to her woodshedding over the tortuous Chaconne.

Instead this version of her had replaced the one everyone knew. My father was not a sophisticated music listener, but she had been sending him such noise for years. For him, these *were* letters. Each note relayed something, perhaps a memory. He tilted his head and listened with the same focus as when he sat by her side during daily practices. I was not around for those, it was none of my business, and classical music bored me. My image of those sessions were now solely from his book, as they were for those who read it, and what people knew of him, as he portrayed himself, had been transposed onto what they saw of him in real life, those passages where patience slowly transmuted into a kind of love.

The sun pierced the cloud cover. Cars shifted lanes.

"Watch it here."

The junction ramps had been switched in the last few months, forcing two streams of traffic to cut into each other with little runway to maneuver. During the afternoon rush hour, this happened as every car was driving straight into the sun. The other day my father was almost sideswiped by a pickup shooting across four lanes at once.

We made it out of that trap and turned north along the length of the valley. Sentinel ridges loomed to either side, yellowing foothills to the east, a darker range to the west, keeping out urbanites and the marine layer. One lone mountain dominated the eastern sky, and although it could be seen clear from the coast, it was not a spectacular sight. In the summer and smokey autumns, it blended into the haze, and it was only occasionally in winter, when it was dusted by snow in the crisp air, that one really saw it.

Baseball fields, sycamore, birch, and juniper populated a vast garden laid out according to the geometry of office parks.

Out of the blue rain began to pour. Another car flashed into the windshield. I swerved, and the car hydroplaned. My first thought was that my father and I were going to die together. When it occurred to me we were still alive, logic took over, underscored by the Pythagorean modulations of my sister's violin. I tried steering the lithe compact through traffic by directing its drift, letting up on the accelerator without slamming on the brakes, which would have sent us into a tailspin. This must have been effective, because the car lost momentum and slammed into the right-hand guardrail at relatively low speed, without triggering the airbags. The damage, I was to discover later, only involved a smashed headlight, a dent, and sidelong scratches.

In another scenario, my father would be the one in the driver's seat. He might have been listening to the same music. He would have no memory of it, because he would be dead, but later inspection would reveal the car had plowed straight into the median divider on the other side of the highway.

In this quantum reality, however, he came out of the crash with only a sore neck. I had no injuries besides my nerves. My

father being a nonbeliever in superstition of any kind, the accident delivered him no message regarding his retirement, but it
did put him off automobiles for a while.

{3}

ONCE HE DETERMINED HE WOULD NOT BE RIDING IN A CAR, the tale shifted to that of the filial son who took up the cause of justice from his predecessor; furthermore, it would be at my father's insistence, for he had taken Ms. Hu's suggestion to heart, that Yvonne Fung see for herself the conditions that had led to Rafael's demise. I would drive, an injunction consistent with his character, how he lent his hand to anyone who sought it and how, once he was no longer able to provide, seeing no problem with offering his son in his stead. He convinced me it was not only my duty to escort Ms. Fung to wherever it was she needed to go for her research, it would be for my own edification. Since we were to share a car together for hours, he said, I had better familiarize myself with the range of her writing, referring me to a volume from her early period, when she was still a university student; then the one that established her reputation; and finally one of her recent, ignored novels, composed after she had relocated to America. Of the first book, I agreed with Ms. Hu's assessment. It was autobiographical, but in an eccentric way that was self-referential to the point of opacity, probably deliberately so. The second book was as she described as well, a complete turnaround from the first. The use of chuánqí in the title, meaning "legend" or a fantastic tale, is likely ironic. Far from being fanciful, the little stories composing the volume were stark; it must have had taken great discipline, perhaps learned from the haunting experiences she described, to be so detached by writing against one's impulses. There was no need for decoration, not about *this* subject, like all the other books about that time, which seemed to share the same ground tone, suggesting a conspiracy of agreement regarding events that could not possibly cohere. Her last one was set in San Mateo, also autobiographical, the only book she had published in years.

"Every time I read something about America by someone who's not an American, they get it all wrong. It's irritating. Of course that includes myself. It's not that I think those books of mine are trash. It's that I don't think about them at all. Sometimes I wonder if the best thing about them is that they helped make me a better businesswoman."

It sounded like a practiced line, something the adult Rimbaud would have used to throw a credulous colleague or journalist off the scent. As for not being an American, was that something so ineffable, I wondered, thinking as an American. Gazing out the windshield, I tried placing myself in a landscape devoid of context: how much of this could I definitively say was *not* China? The straight gables, clapboard construction, and machine-plowed precision of the crop rows suggested as much; likewise, the smell in the air that was neither smoky nor gamey enough, nor drenched in time enough. On the other hand, the sense of space was there, the big land and insistent, feeble attempts to control it. No, this wasn't China, but, for a few details, it could be, by dint of the distances and shifts in perspective here and there.

Now she was in that landscape, separated from me by a windshield splattered with bugs, another reason to find a gas station, and I was losing sight of her in the lettuce fields. We had smelled it from the highway, as our windows were rolled down, but in the fields it was overwhelming, pungent deep-green vegetable and earth. She moved toward an old ranch house on the horizon, having, it seemed, only now to have noticed it. Besides the agriculture, the house was the sole sign of human hand, and there were no other markers for this country. I thought of how *The Grapes of Wrath* was really a Chinese novel, the land money, with people intriguing over every inch of it. One could only imagine what still went on over water and fences. With her eye for property, would she be able to assess value in those spaces, treating the mountains that guided the highway as only another kind of wall? Or was that only an alternate self of hers out there?

Returning to the car, smelling of salad and shoes caked in mud, but somehow managing to remain impeccable in beige suit, red scarf, and gold jewelry, she commented she could not see the mission even from higher ground. She took off the dark glasses she had been wearing the entire drive, although the skies had been overcast, with a bit of rain, and I could see underneath that she bore a superficial resemblance to the book-jacket photo. It was not so much the similarities that impressed me, but the story of the life that had come after the picture was taken, written on those features, turning them into something altogether different, whether due to money and success, thanks to a new career, or an old career, or, as she had implied in her best-known work, to staring into the abyss of human nature, in the heat of revolution.

Imagine, for example, the amazement of the first arrivals of the city youth to the countryside. She had taught the peasants what she knew of chemistry to increase productivity, learned from a childhood on a farm outside Kaohsiung. It won her respect, but life here was still disorienting. She spent those soundless days mostly at a desk, with only a jar of hot water to keep her company, staring out the window at a plot of grass, not quite what in America they call a lawn. The campus was built up a hillside. From the classroom she could see the slope, covered in shrubbery, cutting a slice of pie into the sky. The hill provided shade to the classroom in the afternoon.

The children were moving up and down it, carrying scythes. This scene would weigh on her in later years. She couldn't pin any of her memories down to a single moment. There was only a succession of them, repeated until they turned into one.

In the streets were ancient city walls overgrown with vegetation. People broke off pieces of the vine-eaten, fourteenth-century brick, still stamped with the names of their manufacturers, having withstood, among other things, the Taipings and the Japanese, and used them to build their own walls and braziers. Although the enclosure at times offered a sense of security, other times it generated the sense of being trapped, and the truth was that all of them were trapped, here, in this city known, for its hot summers, as one of the "four ovens." The trees helped, but at the height of the fervor, there seemed a concerted effort to cut them down, to rid the country of nature too, once and for all.[1]

"So why are you writing about this?"

"Everyone complains my books are just transcriptions of my diary, but the truth is, I work hard at making them up. This time, though, I want to try actual reporting. Who knows, it might turn out to be a novel again, but I followed the whole story in the news, and the ending they gave us was unsatisfying, in a manner of speaking; they canceled the show just as it was getting good, and I want to know how it turns out. Your father feels the same way."

I understood the rigor she was bringing to the project when she told me she had gone straight to the court records and found something the Chinese newspapers, for all their obsession with salacious detail, had missed, probably because it did not fit their preconception of Rafael's lover as a kept woman and femme fatale. It turned out she had worked at an airline, and, as of her day in court, was still employed there. It would be easiest to start our search for this woman there, Yvonne explained, since she had otherwise covered her tracks well and left little else to go on. Even Rafael's closest confidantes had not known of her existence. The only thing, she went on, with a disarming smile, was that novelists did not just send emails or make calls to confirm the facts. They had to immerse themselves in the scene. We would do the same.

---

[1] From *Legends of the Great Proletarian Revolution* (Wúchǎn jiējí wénhuà dàgémìng de chuánqí) by Yvonne Fung, a collection of short stories based on her firsthand experience of the early years of the Cultural Revolution.

I told her I had my job to do too, namely stop by the pre-press operation in order to communicate my father's intentions. They were already known, but doing so in person, with myself as intermediary, was part of my father's old-fashioned manners. Yvonne was fine with that. After all, Rafael's business had been the daily reality of most of his life, and she was curious to see it.

The drive back to the freeway went by faded main streets of wooden storefronts and hand-painted signs that had somehow remained immune to the wild speculation in retirement and vacation homes just a few miles away.

Her presence manifested itself, beside me in the car, in her voice. Because we sat facing the same direction, we could not talk directly to each other, but only at an angle, and even though the scenery along the highway was often dull, our minds were distracted by looking at something other than our interlocutor. That slanted focus, both transfixed and scattered, reminded me of something, something that was uncomfortable to be in the presence of and that should not be out in the open like this. What was she doing, I realized, if not composing? Her mind, both coming together and coming apart, had been putting into place neither scenes nor story, which were too fluid to hold their shape in these conditions, but the exact words and sentences, as she looked out the window.

Santa Barbara was a watered-down version of a walled city: turrets and tiles and an underlying mysticism that made it seem more grandiose than it was. The rest spilled out in the narrow edge between a wild mountain range and a brilliant blue channel. Driving with the windows down, we took in the salty wind, which now felt cooler than it had been on the road from Santa Maria. We must have been heading toward the ocean and would reach it if we just kept going in this direction. The city was not so large that we would find ourselves anywhere else.

Yvonne picked up her phone. Who was she talking to? She introduced herself and seemed to be getting directions.

"This is near where they found him." We arrived at the shoreline, perhaps the last thing Rafael saw, a stretch of grass, palms, picnic tables, and barbecue grills, before the sand began, followed by the ocean. The sun was high this time of day, the colors washed out. In one direction oil rigs rose from the horizon. In another, in the haze, like an alien continent, rose the shadows of the closest islands. We were mostly left alone, just some joggers and skaters in knee pads and helmets, some background noise from bars and restaurants on the pier.

Surprisingly, Rafael's final moments seemed of little interest to her. Or they were, but she had gone about it another way. Perhaps she had already carved out this scene, with full attention placed on, say, the sound of the waves. As for the thoughts of the man who led a modestly successful and stable life, neither of us could get anywhere close to that, whichever way we took. If anyone was qualified to speak for him, it would have been my father, but even he probably only knew Uncle Rafael superficially, as a collection of tics, combined with the same old stories others told about him, the ups and downs of his business, an embarrassing midlife love affair, and the ambitions he had abandoned, the way we turn our best friends into caricatures in conversation. Their friendship did not extend beyond that and certainly not to acts of desperation. Those shocking actions, replayed by old friends as best they could in order to make sense of them, might have been perfectly in keeping with the private man he had become.

My father should have been the one here, if only to restore his own sense of order. Over the years I had come to understand that order was not always better than its lack and not what strivers like the woman named Lena Wu wanted, or even winners like Yvonne Fung, but most people otherwise needed it.

At night, the roads were hard to navigate. There were not enough streetlights and no moon. At every turn seemed to be the ocean. It had been a long day, started in what had been a very different setting. I did not think we would uncover much once I found out all Yvonne had to go on was a woman working at an airport. She thought I was just being filial to go on this trip, and was therefore naïve, but I did not think of myself as particularly filial, and I liked to think I let on less than I really knew. We passed the night in a hotel, sharing a room with separate beds, to save money. When I woke, before her, it was light, but not yet warm.

I sat up in bed, pushing aside the pastel bedspread. Right on the other side of the window the freeway had already begun to whir. Beyond that, from the way the horizon bent, was the beach. The parking lot was steamy with fog, the light burning softly through it, not that different from that up north, but more insistent. The diffracted rays sprayed across the ground, the water, and the pale stucco.

{4}

In China it was important not to write anything down. This was not just for fear of having it discovered or confiscated, although, yes, the entire country was engulfed by fear. There was also the sense that writing was action, decisive and irrevocable, and at the time, it was important not to make any sudden moves; therefore, everyone kept a tight rein on themselves. "Look straight into one's own heart," as Confucius once put it. Why writing, in particular among the arts and all the actions one could take? I have my theories. For one, unlike in the West, traditional Chinese culture does not associate the written word with sophistry, but something like its opposite; for another, it does not harbor the illusion that fiction is somehow not the truth.

I spent my days sitting at a desk while the children were out, assembling the pieces of the book in my head, substituting one sentence choice for another, pieces I kept suspended in my mind for years. It was the only book I composed this way, and it was only after I left the country that I got it all down. Once I did, I transcribed it as fast as I could. Some pieces that had been superimposed in my memory all that time became set in what felt like an arbitrary sequence and fixed that way forever.

By the time I got to America, everything I just said about writing became the reverse. Here, one must keep moving all the time. This suits me better personally, but writing here is stasis. The consequences of it are easy to predict: there are none. This makes it hard to keep at, something that dissolves the moment it is put into words. There are plenty of better things to do, actually, and I do not have to keep carrying around anything in my head. When the time comes, I just make it up, which is convenient, but can be in its own way a pain in the ass.[2]

ACCORDING TO MY FATHER, the prepress company did not have a sign, so our best bet was to find the Chinese restaurant adjacent to it. It would not be hard to spot, since it was no hole in the wall, but one of those new tinted-glass monstrosities that had sprung up like giant algae blooms in the desert. Simple enough, but once we arrived in central LA, which lay under a brown film, I found the transition from downtown to the teeming eastern valleys confusing. As we tried to work our way back to the freeway, we wound inside a grid of sun-bleached warehouses, diagonally intersecting roads of windowless distribution centers turning into two-lane boulevards lined by one-story structures of no discernible theme: residences, motels, and little shops. Unmarked buses stopped at unsigned street corners, discharging passengers who dragged their luggage across the too-wide streets in a way that suggested they would not be making the return trip. Cars, speeding too fast, swerved around them.

The further we drifted from the ocean, the heavier with humidity the air grew, taking on an almost tropical character at the

---

[2] Ibid (2nd ed.), afterword.

base of the hills. The palms now grew so tall, even out of traffic islands, that their heads curved out of view from the windshield. After one interminable block after another, strip malls began to dot the landscape, followed by the Chinese language, floating past as channel letters and pylon signs. I was dismayed to find multistory glass structures taking up what I had expected to be a sprawling parking lot; there seemed only curbside parking spaces encircling the mall, but then Yvonne spotted an entrance for an underground garage. An elevator, a sign indicated, would bring us into the restaurant. She suggested that once we made it inside, we could navigate our way back outdoors to look for Uncle Rafael's business. Such circuitousness seemed to be the only means to find one's way around here.

At one point, I had given up, no regrets. In fact, it had made me quite happy, but now I found that strange emptiness return, things spinning out of the air and going back to the air. I had convinced myself there wasn't much to this story, just the sordid affair of a failed businessman, really, but already I could tell there were too many questions to ask. For the first time I could remember, I hesitated in the middle of a book. I knew that if I called it off, nobody would care, not my editor nor my publisher and certainly not my "readership," none save perhaps for this young man and his father, whose motives were extraliterary.

For all the alienation I had felt in China, and it was extreme, it had been experienced—as everything was insisted upon being—collectively. This time was different. It was only the second time, the first being in China, that I found it hard to write. Why? Was this one of those dark, preparatory periods, in which one must drink in experience, in order for it to be properly recollected later? My lesson of China seemed to suggest this. Or was it its opposite, the working out of what had already been written, my living out one of my previous novels? This was the magic that had drawn me to the profession in the first place, when it was the only way to control my life. Or was this just one of those times in which I didn't have the luxury of mind to write, as when my business caught traction and began growing on its own (thank god) and the writing didn't come anymore—and never really did again? One can never say how much money or leisure is needed.[3]

The entranceway to the low-slung building was marked by concrete pavers ringed by ice plants, leading to automatic sliding doors of one-way glass. Coming out to meet us in the reception lobby was a woman in a metallic-green business suit, who was, I knew because I was acquainted with the other, *not* the widow and owner. Behind her trailed three men in white lab coats whose body language told me everything else I needed to know, that she must have been the newly appointed general manager. Speaking to Yvonne, who could not hide her amusement, she explained the lab coats were an affectation of Rafael's. Everyone was required to wear one, even the receptionist, all except for herself and her husband. Rafael, the name he insisted his employees call him, had been a stickler for process and detail—"You will see, you will see"—and the coats, their whiteness and air of rigor, appealed to him. The truth was, she thought they made their operation look dated, but she did not want to shake things up too fast. The staff had grown oddly

---

[3] From *The Lost Lives of Lena Wu* (Wúlìnà shīqù de rénshēng) by Yvonne Fung, introduction.

attached to the coats, as they had to the man who made the rule to wear them. It all sounded so out of character to me; Rafael had struck me as a dreamer, typical of his generation, gentle and spacey, not a despot about dress code and "process," but that may have just been the avuncular persona he put on for children.

Helen, as she introduced herself, took us through a keypad-coded door into a room of what appeared to be highly special-ized, almost medical-looking equipment being worked on by a dozen people in those lab coats.

"He believed that context, more than anything, includ-ing people, affected outcome and quality," she said, speaking in sharply bitten-off syllables, "so he became very concerned that work be done under optimal conditions. In his last years, more and more of his efforts and investment went toward con-trolling this environment as exactly as possible."

Monitors extended from tempered-glass cases like curi-ous animal heads, displaying images of silverware and exercise equipment glamorized for gourmand and fitness magazine covers. A bed-size scanner ran its spidery light over a poster of a motorcycle, its operators sharing the same expression, both fearful and blank. As a production artist zoomed in and out of one of the pictures, I leaned over, to get a better look at her adjusting the shape of a single pixel.

"Everything in this room, as you can see, is white. The lighting is set at a specific frequency for the same reason, so color correction can be done against the most neutral back-ground. Airflow and humidity are strictly controlled in order to minimize free-floating dust, and a false floor was installed in order to cover exposed wiring and ventilation that can attract and produce particulate matter."

She pointed down. Under our feet was a grid of three-by-three-foot white tiles that seemed made of a synthetic material, whose soft edges formed a vacuum seal.

"The wiring and ventilation are invisible, because they're running under us. These panels comprise the most delicate part of the entire operation and had to be custom-made in Japan. For months he traveled across the ocean in order to study prototypes, as well as traditional Japanese homes, which this room resembles, if you think about it." She stopped to breathe. "It puts me in a state of awe whenever I walk through this facility. Of course each special feature is something to admire in of itself, but more impressive, if you ask me, is the total concept. Once you grasp that, it all fits together. He didn't stop at the conceptual level, though. From there he went on to make sure every detail was executed precisely to his specifications. He possessed a rare combination of always thinking ahead, but also being methodical and patient. The one thing he wasn't much for, I'm afraid, was business. Business is basic, even dummies like me get it, but it was the simplest things that tripped him up. If you look at this now, it's sad. It was all a huge mistake."

The heads of everyone were bent over their work. Nobody said anything. The only sound was the breath of the machines.

"It all looks very efficient," I commented.

From what I knew of Rafael's background, the origins of his obsession for detail could be traced to the language he studied and apotheosized in a previous life, predating the entrepreneur. After having been introduced, he joined my father at the newspaper where my father worked to support himself. They were both engineers with literary aspirations; in their respective roles at the student-run magazine they organized, Rafael played the young critic, egging his peers on to attain standards he alone could judge. At the newspaper, he did paste-up, running columns of Chinese typesetting through a wax roller machine and applications of rubber cement, then solving the pages like a puzzle. Sometimes, to change a character, my father or Rafael would scratch out a line, instead of printing out a new word. Columns of text were replicated, spliced, and reordered into new configurations of meaning. That man from my father's stories more resembled this one Helen was glorifying than the one who had disgracefully made the headlines. He was the one who knew this language, the one that came out of the sky, the *only* one, in his mind, capable of truth. Its words could not suffer a single stroke in the wrong place, lest they mean something else entirely, nor the removal of one that might invent a meaning that did not previously exist.

An awareness swept over me as I walked by those stations, as I observed each one of the technicians, as if I had known them and I had been the man who had perished. This was all that was left of him, it occurred to me, and it also occurred to me that Yvonne might not understand his predicament. She was not that sort of businessperson, but rather what she once used to accuse others of being, an opportunist. The other method, which Rafael exemplified, was to purify, the pressure of which could break anyone. Besides the financial factors, setting oneself up as the sole interpreter of rectitude would make everyone else seem a usurper.

In Yvonne's designation, this was how Rafael's widow saw Helen and her husband. There had been ugly scenes involving the three of them with her son, taking place in front of the workers. Was his mother trying to turn him against them? Yvonne believed she must have told him he would take over one day. Helen and Victor of course did not consider him ready, because he was just a kid. In comparison to Yvonne, who had once devoted her life to altering the course of humankind, or my father, who did the same in his own way, these battles were as trivial as they come. If Yvonne managed to make it all sound like imperial court intrigue, that was to her benefit, but at the same time she must have known such a facile portrait would hardly sustain her novelistic needs.

We ended the tour in Helen's office, where her husband, Victor, joined us. By my guess, they were both in early middle age, Victor pasty-faced and taciturn, the younger-looking of the two, Helen taller, certainly more engaging, but somehow less charming. From their wariness of me, I could tell they saw my father as a threat, in a situation rife with them, although probably he was one of their lesser concerns. Altogether, Victor explained, the operation ran around a hundred people, give or take some temp or part-time staff. Business, however, was not good. I pointed out that contradicted what my father had told me.

"Of course Rafael had to be an optimist," he replied, muttering under his breath in a way that contrasted with his wife's strident speech patterns, "especially after making all that investment in the plant. That's probably what your father was going off of, but the reality is the premium services we offer are old-fashioned. They won't say it to your face, but our clients do not care for this level of thoroughness," he gestured toward the keypad-coded door. "They can't tell the difference. That was not what Rafael thought. He believed it all came down to total human effort. You can see that in the lab. His mistake was listening to his customers, while the whole time they were going with the cheaper competition. He finally understood that in the end. We went over all this, of course, but he was a proud man. This business has to change or it will die. There's just not enough work. We tried talking to Margaret about it too, but she's not ready to listen."

Yvonne asked if the widow had visited since her husband's death. She had, he replied, and it had helped. Everyone was just glad to see the family had not abandoned them. Of course people quit, sensing unwelcome changes, but not as many as you might think, and some he had managed to talk into staying, even though their loyalty was clearly to their old boss. It had been hard, not to mention deceptive, reassuring them things were going to carry on as before.

In their guileless, childlike way, Helen and Victor were not good at small talk and the conversation trailed off into silence as they continued to closely observe us. My father's instincts had been mostly right. If he could not be here himself, sending me had smoothed things over, preparing the way for whatever next steps

She remembered how, upon her first, spectacular descent from the air, she saw LA's central grid, which seemed like a sheet of graph paper laid over what it represented, in exact one-to-one correspondence. To a newcomer like herself in a window seat, the sight of it stretch-

he had in mind, the same method he had employed against Ms. Hu. These were the inconvertible tools of diplomacy: respects paid, greetings given, courtesies received, and gestures made, even if one knew nothing immediate would come of them. But it was also true nobody paid mind to conduct anymore, and propriety went against the grain of this country. Perhaps out of that alien impulse, Helen and Victor invited us to dinner, mentioning we could wait in one of the meeting rooms while they finished up, but we replied with the same false courtesy.

We needed to go to the airport, Yvonne said, and should get going if we were going to beat the traffic.

ing from the desert to the ocean wouldn't have the same impact as it would later, as someone who had been down there and lived it. Nor would the next opportunity come soon. In fact, the scale and system of Southern California only revealed itself to her after she landed. Whether because of the width of the roads, which were straight as geometry, or the lack of height of the structures along them, the buildings did not, as they did in Taipei, close in around her. Instead they shrank away. Because of this sense of continuously riding the crest of a wave, the view, while not that from a plane descending, was somehow aerial.

The days passed until she no longer felt like a foreigner, confined by the odd hours of the airport, where it was neither day nor night. Instead she now saw the day as it was spent, the movement of the sun, the changes in wind and temperature. She ignored the dreams of that other life as she walked on dissolving sidewalks and past untended gardens. The front door of her second-story one-bedroom

My father had long propounded two notions that I always found troubling. One, which went against our modern grain, was that simplicity almost always deserved condemnation, while complexity, by definition many-sided, allowed for a more nuanced view. In his mind, a fraud passing himself off as honorable might win some crumbs of dispensation, thanks to that honor, however opened onto a shared balcony with a view of a curb lined with cars. If she leaned over the rail a little more, she could catch a glimpse of the sea. Further out were long sections, transitional neighborhoods with no look. In Taiwan they would have been called the countryside.

At this moment, her life lay in a delicate balance; a single decision could change her fate. If she went back, she would find herself in the same predicament, only worse, because, if it were possible, she would be even poorer. The only thing for sure was if she did nothing.[4]

false, but a boor who did not cloak his shortcomings deserved no sympathy. He did not care for those who "tell it like it is."

The other was the idea, generally agreed upon among his generation although becoming less so by mine, of a just man always being alone, surrounded by active and passive conspirators working against him.

I could not help seeing a contradiction. Is there any stock character more simplistic than that of the wronged and isolated man fighting for justice, in vain? This contradiction, or combination, also seemed susceptible to authoritarianism; once you whittled away the simpletons and conspirators, you would be left only with those who could afford to be "individuals."

---

[4] Ibid.

This outlook was what made him suspicious of Helen and Victor, blinding him to their efforts to be responsible. His old age, meanwhile, placed the emphasis on *conspiracy*, his conviction that they had some prior agreement with Lena Wu. Such actions were tantamount to murder, even though, as I had pointed out to him, there had been no evidence they had even been aware of each other's existence prior to the incident.

Recent events, the growing rift between them and Margaret, for example, lent some credence to his theories, but now it was my job to follow the thread to Lena and from there to the man who actually pulled the trigger. Lena, though, I believed would be enough: again without evidence, my father thought the perpetrator had been manipulated the whole time by his paramour.

"Your father may be half right," Yvonne opined. So far she had withheld judgment during our long drive, while I relayed my father's theories. It was all part of her compositional method, keeping eyes and ears and mind open, etc., but now she came out with this: "Helen and Victor are conspirators against the throne, *but* not with Lena, rather with . . . Rafael himself." He had been plotting to take his own company from himself? "Hear me out." Seeing the plant and meeting Helen and Victor in person had corroborated her suspicion that Rafael must have been his own worst enemy. Lena was the one who would have been in the best position to see this and the only one who might get through to him. When he ignored even her, insinuating that she was trying to work an angle, she gave up on him.

The company she found a collaborator to help her take over was the one Rafael had originally envisioned. But that had been by another self, from another time.

There was no reason to think he did not change his mind about everything he had worked for. He had come to a conclusion he could arrive at only if he considered it deeply enough.

"It's just a story I came up with," she added, dismissing everything she had just said. On the one hand, I thought, the scenario was consistent with my father's other disconcerting belief, that in any situation self-interest would always play a stronger role than passion. Assuming Rafael's enemies were contemptible, they could not have any more complicated motives than might be explained by the most simplistic. But, I wondered, was an elaborate conspiracy more or less complicated than a messy crime of passion? How fine a difference was there between a worldview that said people were *mostly* motivated by self-interest versus one saying they were *only* motivated by it? It was worth noting that, in my father's field of work, the answers to mysteries were almost always the most outlandish ones.

"I admit the lab coats were a screwy touch," I said.

"You didn't find it disturbing? How sheeplike everybody was?"

"That seemed more to be Helen than anything else. She's got them under her heel. Look, maybe we've got it all wrong. I mean, would *business differences* make you want to shoot somebody, even fake it?"

"It could have been over anything. It could have been over a dust speck. He was pretty crazy about them!"

"Honor, maybe?"

"The story of a failed businessman is no story at all."

The temperature cooled as we drove into the sun. Out-of-date but still cheery billboards and what was left of drive-ins that were now walk-up taquerías appeared to the side of the road. What filled the long stretches of office complexes that seemed more extensive than possibly necessary? It was impossible to imagine all of them being occupied, and yet, if they were empty, they would seem somehow even more monumental.

I had gone to the plant so I could tell my father that I had. I had not thought to find anything there. What I discovered was a man's lifework. Would he have turned his back on it so easily? Did Helen and Victor understand that, by saving it, they were only accelerating its failure? No, Rafael was probably not crazy. The results, maybe, were deformed, but the vision was true, pragmatic even. We would have to take a look into the books, something, I was sure, my father would do.

Yoshinoyas glowed from the edges of the avenues. I had never seen so many. I had eaten in one before, but that had been in Taiwan, not here.

"They're not like they are in Taiwan," Yvonne said.

It made us both crave authentic Taiwanese food, which was hard to find up north. Meanwhile I was losing direction. We seemed to be moving further from the ocean. On

the court record Lena Wu had said she could see the ocean from her window, but that could have been anywhere on the coastline. The air had the quickness of the coast, so maybe we were not drifting too far away.

The days were terrifying, because she owned them entirely now. In this city where everything going on in the world was going on inside of it as well, one should never be short for opportunities, but she allowed herself to remain unfixed, imagining such passivity would allow her to drift somewhere else, when

I thought of the main character in Yvonne's book, at one with the landscape. There were fewer trees inland, no shadows in its searing light.

You could see a long way, but it was too much area to cover for a single person. If she were still in the city, even as big a one as Los Angeles, Yvonne would be able to find her, but out there, in the rest of the state, possibilities decompressed all the way to the border. If we kept going this way, even as the barren land receded and expanded toward the horizon, the freeways grew narrower. Everything would end in a knot of buildings, train tracks, walkways, parking lots, and steel walls.

instead she only found herself repeatedly circling back to the same landmarks. Should she stay in the apartment, which was a quadrant on that sheet of graph paper no better or different than any other quadrant? Or get in the car and press the gas pedal? It seemed she could find all the answers in her little square, in the dark, rather than looking in other, lit squares.

She might have stayed put, too, if she had not been pushed out by a chunk of her ceiling caving in. She lay there in bed, staring up at the hole, with slivers of the apartment above visible through it, while her apartment flooded. Her landlord offered her a temporarily open unit in another complex. Because of this, she began to get to know the part of the city closer to the ocean, going past the dried-out lawns and palm trees growing out of the sidewalk and situating herself, via her reflection, in glass homes designed to be looked into. The beach didn't call out to her, but she liked to take her time in the border alleys that ran behind oceanfront property.

In the other direction, away from the sea, she discovered, almost by accident, blank neighborhoods marked only by Chinese signs. She found herself entering a breakfast joint, next to a gas station, where retirees spent their mornings over newspapers and soy milk. It should have been a kind of homecoming, but at this point, she had been away long enough that, even if her memory were jogged, she could not tell if the food she was tasting fell short of expectations. It was also possible the target of her nostalgia no longer existed, that this was all there was now. The rest was just in her head, no longer a memory and something closer to fiction.

The old people were not shy about striking up conversation, which would have been perfectly normal back home. There was no reason to think they were not in Taipei now, no matter the street view outside. They asked her what neighborhood she was from, and with a question or two, they came up with names they knew in common. One person knew, or had heard of, her family. She responded politely, to let them know she had been raised properly. The streets were dusty, the sun bleak. Looking to the east, or what she thought of as east, she tried imagining how long this went on repeating itself. The desert, for someone from a green, tropical island, was as alien as anything.[5]

5 Ibid.

{5}

AIRPORTS ARE THEIR OWN COUNTRY, more like one another than the cultural and natural worlds in which they reside, with hallways wide enough to drive through and the most interesting parts off-limits. Even by these standards, this one had a particularly anodyne aspect; nevertheless, Yvonne was fascinated to see where Lena had spent her days, more fascinated than she had been by Rafael's laboratory.

She wondered aloud if Lena preferred to spend her first months in a new country in this place that was neither one nor the other. For the discombobulated group shuffling out of customs, this might be their first glimpse, up close, of the real thing, after a lifetime of seeing it on TV and the internet; and so, even if Lena considered the airport to be nothing more than an office she clocked into every day, albeit one of massive proportions, where one sunless day blended into all the others, it would still recover its novelty so long as she was able to see it through the eyes of its perpetual stream of newcomers.

"It may be their first glimpse," I pointed out, "but I doubt it makes much of an impression. For many of them, it's just a matter of getting past the checkpoints and hoping they never come back again."

"You'd think it wouldn't, but it does, in particular the colors, the smells, the weight of the air. These stayed with me, as other details faded. Even if you don't ever want to come back, you don't forget. You can't go back, anyway. You only get to experience it once."

Like my father, who never spoke to me of that arrival or the difficult days which followed it, she had once been a newcomer too. I had momentarily forgotten that; it was true I no longer thought of her as one of those entering through those steel doors. Much of this project seemed to consist of blanks in Lena's experience being filled by Yvonne's rich memories. I had not thought we needed to come here; the things that needed asking could have been requested in other ways. At the time I thought it was because we agreed greater truths could be derived face-to-face, with expressions and gestures that communicated as much as, if not more than, words, but I remembered now the novelist's task. We were not here to gain information, per se. We were to leave Yvonne's head somewhere in this place and let it find its way around.

The place, as it turned out, was the food court, where Maisie, frizzy-haired and panda-eyed, entered in uniform. On first impression she seemed she could have somehow been either Lena's closest friend or her worst enemy. We formed a triangle around a circular table, Maisie with a plastic carton of salad, her dinner for the night, while Yvonne and I were content drinking coffee out of cardboard cups. It seemed it might be detrimental to her work, but Maisie possessed the slow, measured air of someone accustomed to being waited on, rather than the other way around. Right off the bat she admitted she and Lena had not been on good terms.

Actually, everyone hated her in Taoyuan, she explained. This was before both of them had been sent Stateside. Lena had earned a reputation for shamelessness among the ground crew rank and file. Everyone knew she only cared about getting assignments for the VIP lounge in order to meet the most promising prospects, and the only way to do that was to cozy up to their supervisor, who himself was in an unhappy marriage to a sick wife. Maisie did not know how it happened, but Lena must have miscalculated at some point, because instead of hooking a big fish from the lounge, she ended up marrying their humble supervisor—though not before breaking up his family.

Yvonne did not keep notes, not openly with a pen or recorder, anyway. Instead she seemed to be slowly taking in Maisie's words, situating them in that remarkable memory of hers, then rearranging them, in various layouts, even as Maisie spoke. We did not know Lena was married.

In fact, Maisie continued, it was the stupid politics of it all that got her transferred after Lena had the run of the place. Once installed as the new wife, she went about sidelining the competition. Maisie, on the other hand, was more than happy to leave all that drama behind. She was just starting to enjoy her new life when she found out Lena and her husband were moving to LA. Yes, they had followed her here. Of course she expected the worst, but somehow, whether because they were now all strangers together or because it was a smaller crew, which forced them to rely on one another, the couple's bad behavior had not made the trip with them. In fact they all ended up friends, although not so much Lincoln, from whom she had always kept some distance. Nor was it exactly uncomplicated with Lena. Something had come over her since she arrived. Perhaps their marriage had already been shaky by the time they got here, but Maisie got the impression Lena was not taking the transition well and therefore clung to the only other person from her past life besides her husband.

In response to Yvonne's question about children, she said Lincoln had a daughter, from the first wife, who was around the same age as Lena. That had been part of the scandal too.

Maybe they were happy after all, but put it this way, when Maisie found out Lena was mixed up in that business, which she believed was what we were here for, she was not surprised.

That may not have been the response Yvonne wanted to hear; nevertheless, she pressed on, asking if it was true she had been having an extramarital affair.

One never knew. She may have just got caught up in the internecine politics of a family business. Maisie knew about predicaments like that. They got nastier than anything, with blackmail, murder, you name it. Whatever it was, Lena kept it well hidden, so all there was to see, and therefore what became the truth, resided in the imagination of others.

Lincoln had since retired. He did it after they got divorced. According to the rumor mill, he cashed out the entire package at once and bought a boat with it. Now he ran cruises out of Ventura Harbor.

"You should look him up. He runs ads in the local Chinese papers."

"Are you still in touch with him?"

"No, I was never close to him, which was a good thing."

As for his ex-wife, that would be harder. Maisie had heard she moved out to the desert, but that was something you heard about anybody who left LA. In fact she was driving by the ocean the other day when she realized she was near Lena's old apartment. Out of idle curiosity or subconscious nostalgia she went by to take a look. Surprisingly, a familiar car was parked out front on the curbside, but no sign of the person. Maisie called, but the number was disconnected. Well, actually this was all a few months ago; nevertheless, she could not have gone far, Maisie felt or imagined, and it would not shock her to see her friend show up at the airport one day, behaving as if nothing happened and time had not passed. They would converse as if they were still in Taoyuan, as if they were still bickering rivals.

Maisie gave us the address, and we found ourselves in the neighborhood, if that is the right term for it here. We were surprised by echoes of the Bay Area, similar elements and even people, albeit in different proportions. This latter quality caused things to multiply and repeat, such as the identical-looking apartment complexes, which in turn served as a kind of camouflage. Meanwhile the impermanent nature

Everyone has to start somewhere, blackjack, roulette, craps. Older Chinese men, led by tour operators, came in during the wee hours, stepping up to her table, still on Beijing time. At the airport she'd been a genius of killing time, but now it just flowed and flowed. Her dexterity and single-mindedness made people look at her and think,

of Southern Californian architecture made me wonder if the address still existed among all its doppelgängers. Despite that, persistence, or just continued aimless driving, paid off, and we located at least the address. Was it the same building she had resided in or had it been torn down and a new one put in its place? It was hard to tell. From my car I could spy an open door on the second-floor balcony. Was it hers? Perhaps our luck had held out, and we had managed to catch this one's going places, but she had doubts. You were swimming against the current, and so many were pulled out to sea. Those who thought it all just a matter of achieving the right state of mind were kidding themselves. She was a fast learner, though, a natural. The goal was to blow through this stage as fast as possible, but it soon became apparent the current was dragging her out too. She needed something that could generate its own power. If only she could catch her breath. After years, this was her first real lesson about this country. You thought you were just playing, it lulled you into a slower pace than what was good for you, but what you needed to do was to move faster, make something happen, then make it happen again.[6]

her here, while she was on her way out.

We walked up the floating stairs. Sand covered the steps; things turned to sand in this city faster than anywhere else. She had managed to wipe out almost every trace of herself, so her Rafael's friends would come looking for her. None of them did, yet. She'd covered her tracks. They'd

---

[6] Ibid.

being here now seemed only an acceleration of, not an exception to, that process. Yet, if our timing had worked out differently, we might have caught her just as she was coming down the stairs, leaving behind her apartment for good. Instead, it somehow felt we had just missed her. Or that she had just passed us by, but without being noticed somehow. This was the apartment number Maisie had written down for us. The door hung there, in space, ajar. We pushed it and went in.

grow fainter with time. Things turned to sand in this city faster than anywhere else. She packed boxes and carried them, weighed down by nothing she wanted, into the van. If she'd known she'd be doing everything by herself, which was true even when she was with Lincoln, she'd never have come. It all fit into the vehicle. Her skin was grainy with the salt of the sea air, gritty on the back of her neck and her arms. She allowed herself one last indulgence: a look back at the emptied apartment. A lot had happened here, but she had no good memories. She had been alone. The days just kept going, and she didn't know how to stop them. It had been only her and the gods then, who in their remorselessness taught her how to overcome fear; nonetheless, it had been home. The door was left open. She didn't bother shutting it behind her.[7]

Lincoln stared at the deep-sea tank for what must have been thirty minutes, through its fused, Japanese plexiglass. He wasn't capable of disappointment. They had driven north to stay at the

---

[7] Ibid.

house of a wealthy acquaintance to whom they were introduced by a mutual friend, someone Lincoln was convinced would invest in his boating-company idea. As they arrived from the south, her first shock was the twisting gray cypresses overlooking the ocean and the biting sea wind. The sun was bright but it was cold.

This time, though, it wasn't Lincoln being typically awed. The sights were like nothing they had glimpsed in Los Angeles. In the bay, fat squid kept floating up to the surface, drawing crowds of sea lions and gulls. He was stunned the wild creatures were so close in front of them in such numbers, understandably so, Lena thought, even though no one else seemed impressed, not the other tourists, nor the harbor merchants and fishermen who inexplicably seemed not to know what to do with the hapless mollusks washing up in droves.

He wanted to go down for a closer look. She hung back, because she wasn't wearing the right shoes, choosing to simply marvel at how clean the water was. Neither of them had ever seen anything so blue, like something mineral, and the animals, in their element. She kept waiting for the back of a dolphin to cut through a wave. Somebody claimed to have seen one, but someone else said it was probably just a sea lion or driftwood. The other bystanders also kept away from the water. Because it was cold? She told him not to go onto the rocks. Only gangs of young boys were crawling around out there, and him, a middle-aged man.

Squid filled the ocean to depths past which lay only darkness. It wasn't the aquarium, brightly illuminated by coral, anemone, kelp, and urchin. Even the tidal rocks fell away from view once you looked beyond them, so all that existed, it seemed, was the rays of the sun caught in the water's prism, a gem of cold green, and the squid, at multiple distances, jumping in and out of view. The mirror dissolved each time one of the boys threw a rock into it, each time surprised they didn't hit one of the animals, before settling back into clarity.

They used to sneak off from the airport in Taoyuan to watch the sunsets in Keelung or Tamsui, where he'd buy shells and coral to decorate his apartment with. Back then, their life, as it existed now, was something he'd only talked about. It had been all worked out in his head, and against all expectation it had turned out exactly as he'd said it would be.

A squid, hard to tell how big it was from here, was caught in an eddy, being driven into a pool. She watched it try to keep from washing up onto one of the rocks and swim to open water. The waves pushed it this way and that. Finally Lincoln couldn't stand it any longer. He was always the first one to lose patience. He grabbed a stick and tried moving closer, where he could poke or flip it out over the current, risking life and limb for the invertebrate. She yelled at him to be careful, but he insisted and stretched as far as he could, until he could touch it, but he still couldn't quite push it out.[8]

By what we observed being sold at roadside stands—fresh honeycomb in Tupperware, dulce de leche in glass jars, and in baskets: olallieberry, boysenberry, apricot, nectarine, Valencia oranges, summer squash, papaya, guava, mango—it seemed we had arrived at a place where anything and everything could be harvested and done so year-round. Coming through the rolled-down driver's-side window was the smell of kelp and chum and through the passenger-side was that of freshly turned earth opened to the sun. The two types of air mingled, that of the saline burn of the sea and the milder heat of the valley, and the

------

[8] Ibid.

region seemed to benefit from both or even make of them into something more luxurious.

As we tacked closer to the offshore islands, and they took on more definition than the unsteady shadows that seemed about to dissolve with the morning marine layer, the oceanic aspect came to prominence. Driving toward the pier, which itself jutted from an outcropping, the blue sea seemed to appear ahead, behind, and to the west, while those islands seemed less like floating visions and instead peaks of another continent, as if the sea had narrowed to the width of a channel. We were looking on the pier for Lincoln's cruiser; the name we were told to go by was "007." As we approached what we thought was its berth, we heard some splashing between the boats, which turned out to be an immense sea lion, standing erect from fore-flippers to head as tall as an adult human, making its way out of the water and onto the dock, where it made itself at home.

If it came out a little further, it would have blocked our way. As it was, we were wary of approaching any closer, but then we could see past its shoulder a thin and dark-skinned man, in a white polo shirt and baseball cap, tying down a cabin cruiser so his passengers could disembark. From what I could make out from the Cantonese chatter, they were sightseers from Hong Kong. After they scurried past the large mammal, Yvonne and I approached the captain. He did not know us, we said, yet once we explained our purpose, his mood brightened. We should consider ourselves to be from the same village, he said. Of course Taiwan was much bigger than a village, and Yvonne was from Kaohsiung, while he was from Taipei. I was not even really from Taiwan in the first place, but in the context of where we stood now, Taiwan may as well have been a tiny village and the three of us family.

He was eager to show us his craft. Neither of us were prepared to get on it. Was preparation necessary, or was it no different than getting in a car? In the cockpit hung a framed big-head cartoon sketch, done by a sidewalk artist, of what was recognizably himself as 007 and an Asian woman, possibly Lena, as sexy Bond girl. If it was her, he had not seen fit to take it down.

The next thing we knew we were low down to the water. It was not like being on one of those luxury liners. From this vantage point the ocean was not a flat, blue plain, but a more varied terrain of hills and valleys, and the gods which presided here were not the revolutionary and pragmatic gods of the New World, but the milder ones of classical antiquity, who had somehow rediscovered their Mediterranean here. While it was possible to imagine the Chumash paddling out to the islands, which looked deceptively reachable, it was also possible to see stone columns rising out of the waves as dolphins raced our boat under the clear surface. Yvonne leaned over the stern into a much colder wind than what we felt on shore to get a better look at them and toward brown pelicans just hanging in the air, so close it seemed she could reach out and touch them.

He said he had wanted a boat since he was a child. No, he had not grown up around the fishermen of Keelung or Lukang; anyway, that would not have struck him as desirable. He had been a city kid, so the image of the sea must have been implanted by the movies.

"James Bond?" Yvonne said.

"How did you know? I came out here, talked to some people. I came up with the cash and was in business."

"You found your calling. Sometimes it happens late in life. It happened for me too."

"Writing?"

"No, being a realtor."

"I sail the sea, you sell land." This seemed to please him. "But I barely make enough to get by."

Here with him I felt complicit with what Lena had done, by way of my connection to Uncle Rafael. Even at the time, I realized that did not quite make sense, but why else was I on this trip, if not to make amends for what Rafael did? I wondered, the longer this trip went on, how far my sense of responsibility would go, responsibility, in my mind, being something no different than greed, that is, an extension of the ego. No one, or I could easily imagine no one, had come to this decent-seeming man, who had invited us onto his ship and took great, simple joy in the ocean, and apologized for Rafael's behavior. (I was not thinking of Lena's behavior, although that would have been more on Lincoln's mind.) Things in this world were being left for others to take up, with no sense of obligation or sympathy. As my sister would have pointed out, that was not somebody else's problem, it was mine.

He explained to Yvonne he was the one who did not want kids. He had already been through all that and did not care to do it again. In the end, he wanted to give Lena some space, so he moved, remembering the good times they had out here. He thought she would come around eventually, as she just needed some time to herself, but she never did.

The more I heard about her, the more the callow, younger woman of my first impression, from the newspaper coverage and my father's characterization, seemed to mature. She was probably older than I thought she was, a woman with a work history, who had been married, then divorced. There was still an age gap with him, although it was hard to tell exactly how much—he was fit and dark from the sun—maybe twelve to fifteen years.

He asked if Lena was in trouble. The question puzzled Yvonne. I supposed she could not imagine he had not heard about the scandal, but not wanting to be the one to bring it up, she said it was a money matter. Did he know her current whereabouts? He had lost track of her, he replied, but he had received letters. The first one had been months ago, but another had arrived recently. She left no email or phone number, but there were changing return addresses on the envelopes, written in her hand. He had written back the first time but not after that, he admitted. He could show us the letters, if we did not mind coming home with him.

"We don't want to intrude on your privacy."

"There's nothing in them. You'll see."

"Did she move back to Taiwan?"

"No, they were all from different places in California."

I looked to Yvonne to see what she made of this, but she let on nothing. On land, our legs checked the ground as we took steps away from the harbor. Lincoln stayed back, but pointed toward the interior of the island. "There's a nice view from the top."

There was no shade on the trail, and neither of us had thought to bring a hat. As we moved up the dusty path, pawprints appeared in the dirt, starting abruptly in the middle of cleared ground, then padding into dry, gray-copper brush. From the summit, we could actually see whales, one group and a pair that might be mother and calf. The water glimmered a translucent turquoise in the reefs around the harbor.

As we came down, we picked up speed and paid less attention to the sights, thinking, perhaps, to what lay ahead. At the same time I could not shake the feeling that something was tagging along behind us. When I turned around, my eyes met those of a little gray fox, its head tilted in a pose of curiosity, matching mine.

Your problem is your obsession with real estate. You think location means progress. But location is just dislocation.

Then again I was really happy to hear you finally started your business. You've been talking about that for years. I should have known. I don't know why anybody doubts you at this point. You've proven when you put your mind to it, you make something happen. How many people can say that? Don't take this the wrong way, but I don't think anybody really thought you could pull it off. I think they thought you were kidding yourself, and you were entertaining everybody with your foolishness. Well, maybe I believed you. Maybe it was because you were so damned literal-minded.

Part of me wishes I was there. It sounds like fun. But maybe it also sounds too predetermined for me. After all, it's what you always wanted, right? And an adventure like that, a personal dream, can be scary too.

We had too much to lose, or so we were convinced. At the airline, we just wanted someone to look after us and we had no choice where to go. It didn't take much to snap out of that, but one can fall forever, and I see now as a person who has to live by her wits that everyone is a predator, everything a construct.

I never had any goals. You did. I know all you wanted was to live by the sea somewhere. That was something amazingly concrete. Because I never had any intentions of my own, I went with you. I knew what you wanted, a house that faced the sunset, so that at the end of every day you could look out on how far you'd come. But it's just at that moment, as you settle in to enjoy the view, you see yourself for what you are.

We should not emulate the hermit who exiled himself to the wilderness so he did not have to face the reality of his ability and importance. We should test ourselves.

You didn't have those pretensions. You just wanted your house by the sea. I wanted you to have it.

Anyway, I hope the house works out for you. I realize everything turned out exactly as you imagined it would, except for one thing. As for me, I've gotten used to things not turning out the way I think they will.

What lasts is built out of desperation. There's never any other reason. You see it in all that's left, in these old missions, shacks, and farms around here, the dry grass and trees overlooking the ocean.

Thanks for your letter. I was surprised you wrote back. To be honest, I found it a bit confusing. It sounds weird as I'm writing this, but I wasn't sure to whom you were writing. Half of it, I'm sure, was meant for somebody else, while the other half sounded addressed to me.

We talked ourselves into all kinds of things, didn't we? All that's required is a change of mind to get out of these traps of one's own making. It's something I've been thinking a lot about lately. Not just because of what happened to Rafael, although I wish it'd been something he'd been capable of (changing his mind). For whatever reason, it seems he got more and more entangled in his own misconceptions.

Some of that was nothing but the drudgery of work and what we put ourselves through in order to get through it. So I'm with you so far. But then you make it sound as if the conclusion you've come to is that we're only financial creatures after all, as if that's the end we must come to. I don't know. Isn't it because everything is illusory we must not succumb to money? Civilization, after all, is all we have. Maybe that makes me one of those ancient Chinese I despise, afraid to face his shortcomings, but once I feel we let this go, we let it all go.

Am I looking for justice? When justice becomes an end unto itself, it produces unintended consequences. I think of those policemen I thought were going to help me, but who turned out to have their own agenda. An old story. Justice was once the occupation of the world. It's all well and good until you're the one it turns against.

We're not living in those kinds of times now.

What we want can just be the outcome of correct procedures. That was something Rafael passionately believed in. Did he get it wrong? What happened to him shouldn't have happened. I know things like that aren't random. A person doesn't live right and have something like that happen to them.

The world is full of people I can't take at their word.[9]

---

[9] As promised, when we went to Lincoln's home, he showed us Lena's letters. I can vouch for the existence of at least two of them, having seen them with my own eyes, but I did not read them carefully, as Yvonne did,

---

and of course they were originally written, by hand, in Chinese. I wish to make clear that what I have translated here is not from those originals, but from clippings my father made of the printed edition of *The Lost Lives of Lena Wu*, where the letters are included as part of the Appendix. While the contents of the Appendix roughly correspond to my vague memory of the originals, it does not seem likely that my father would have had access to them, or any verification of their existence, nor is it clear that Yvonne ever had them in her possession, despite her later claim to the contrary, for Lincoln only showed them to us at the time and did not let us take them. As for Lincoln's (and, later, Yvonne's) reference to an unspecified number of letters that seemed to constitute a series, I wonder if this was some kind of misprision on my father's part, who after all was going off his imagination. I only ever saw two, the number of letters included in Yvonne's book, which were in turn appropriated for my father's manuscript. In other words, there is no way for me to find out without contacting Lincoln again what discrepancies, if any, exist between Lena's words and Yvonne's version of them. My father's manuscript now serves as a frame around Yvonne's book, which in turn frames its Appendix; here, the artifice of fiction and the artifice of translation converge, pressing the layers of the palimpsest into one.

{6}

MY SISTER WALKED BY. Lights, low. She already looked heavy, where she had always been slight, someone who had always looked like a kid. Performing was the only time she became a full-size adult, until now.

It was early afternoon in unremitting inland heat. There were eight of us from the Society, including myself. While the others roamed elsewhere, four of us circled the pool, which was edged in brick. Probably nobody swam in it now, even if the water was regularly cleaned. I imagined they might hold performances outdoors, acting scenes on a midsummer night. It would be pleasant, although I could not imagine the plays, which seemed very much the interior type, lending themselves to being performed here. On the other hand, a Noh stage, erected by the pine tree, under the gaze of the mountain, would work perfectly, but they probably did not do that, despite the collection of masks in the foyer and the name of the house.

People commented how she came off as a blank in my father's memoir. It was true, his method was to write around his subject, by adding so much intimate background detail that one could, in effect, see the outline around the empty vessel. He did not tell me one way or the other if this was his intention; simply that much was evident. He did say that, although it was true nothing ever came out the way he meant it to, it was especially so when it came to writing about a child. You could try to get inside the head of one, but you would not find anything there.

Ms. Hu was standing on the back porch. It had been a great effort just to bring her this far out of the city, but she insisted, as part of her new and sudden, and it must be said, very late, interest in American literature, something she had shown no interest in, or really even any awareness of, all her long life, even during all the years she had lived in this country. The valley she looked out on was filled with single-family homes, pools, and trees, but was mostly taken up by yellow patches, which were not earth, but grass. Every window inside the house, I noticed, offered the same view, in the same direction. The house had been designed for people to stare at it, stare at it straight on, at a time when the valley was unpopulated. I imagined it must have been maddening, that rural emptiness, especially since the two of them were city people, although it was said the wife, who was sensitive to light, kept the shades drawn. The grounds in the back of the house sloped down to fences and juniper shrubs that hid the site from the rest of the neighborhood. Down the hill my father wound his way on stepping stones in the garden. From the porch where Ms. Hu and I stood, we could see the whole path by which we had arrived: crossing the old rail track, now a bike trail, then over the freeway by bridge, down the main strip past gas stations and parking lots, to the old train depot, where a van waited to take the Society, the time slot's entire tour group, up the hill on the opposite side of the valley from the mountain. Over our backs rose another range, which made the shadows grow long, and beyond it, through a significant stretch of wilderness, lay, it was weird to think, Oakland.

A pregnant woman, on the other hand, was literally filled in. I could not imagine she enjoyed being so tangible. I heard her steps, down the hall, lumbering. I wondered if her playing would change with thicker fingers. The reality of her, of the here and now, contrasted with the absence in those pages.

I did not read plays, not even Shakespeare. The house, with a second-level wooden portico, was painted white with a black-shingled roof and smaller than I imagined for something bought with Nobel money. But then it was more than enough for two people, even if you counted the servants, who had been sequestered in ground-floor quarters. Meanwhile, the houses of their neighbors kept growing bigger. Even their inhabitants' appetites could not fill them, so most of them sat half empty. I had a friend who carried a walkie-talkie around his house just to stay in touch with his family. Of course people did not really employ servants nowadays, not in that way, so those rooms remained empty too.

My sister said she blew up like a balloon in a few days. The human body is more mutable than we think. Our idea of our physical selves has put us, in our modern minds, in a fixed form. Thus the obsession with weight loss, fitness, etc.

It had been Ms. Hu's idea to convene the next meeting of the Society here, as part of her newfound fascination, but this was Steinbeck country, more or less, wasn't it? The pastoral scenery was not representative of this house belonging to a neurotic collector of Japanese masks. What was the connection between Tao and Noh? There was none. Noh is Shinto, a fact never properly explained to Westerners. There was a culture here after all, although the writer came here precisely to escape from such burdens. Meanwhile, the suburbs grew mindlessly, and this site was lost in them, until somebody remembered. Why not someone we had heard of? There was a replica of Jack London's shack in Oakland. Was Steinbeck's home a national monument? It was not. America did not have its literary priorities straight, nor did it rank its writers with any precision. In China everybody knew who the top three were, in order.

The ancients understood this, with their gross bodily humor and point of view not limited to the unitary viewer, so they could move through nature, birds, clouds, even stones. Now only poets did this, with the flow of their minds.

I felt an urge to go back inside, knowing I would probably never come here again. The sun went down behind the hills we were standing on, and the effect was that everything went prematurely dark, while the valley amphitheater before us glowed, as if from a fire. Down in the walnut orchard, the Society members continued across the grounds, up through the hawthorn beds, around the side of the house, back to the front gate, to the barn and pet dog's grave. Abstracted at this particular distance, the view of the mountain seemed framed, which was no doubt a deliberate design by whomever chose this site. Back on the porch, I retreated to the door from which we had emerged from inside the house.

It was just as it was when we had both lived at home, the four of us around the table, except now the children were both middle aged. My sister said they did not have decent Chinese food where she lived. I was surprised it was important to her. My mother served up lion's head, which is pork meatballs wrapped in cabbage, made from an old family recipe. She was from Yangzhou, city of gourmands, and while she herself was no gourmand, as I could attest, and the lion's head recipe learned against her will, my sister was overwhelmed by its supposed authenticity. My father had fond recollections of Yangzhou, which he and my mother visited on their first and last trip to the mainland. The one disappointment he encountered was the city's most famous dish, fried rice, which he said tasted just like . . . fried rice. The idea of visiting China for him had long been a dream, and although he knew all the sights, it was from writing, not photographs, which did none of it justice. And after he got there, it did not seem right they did not exist only in words. I remembered Yvonne once making a comment in this vein. Was it in person or in her book? For all that, my father admitted the sights were impressive. West Lake's mist and the Great Wall, in a country where everything seemed to be a rip-off, could not be contained by brazen exploitation, which was not the case in America. The country was richer than he thought, not materially. The people, at that time, were still dirt poor, but those scholars had not exaggerated. They knew exactly how to draw a bird or trees. They knew people. In the end, he preferred to leave the Middle Kingdom in his mind and as literature and art. He had had opportunities to go back, but passed.

The mountain reminded me of Yvonne's story of the red-scarved child-locusts defoliating the hill by the school, cutting grass with their scythes. The picture, so precise in my memory, must have come from her book, but maybe she had also referred to it in passing, when she was reliving her experiences in Nanjing during our drive down the coast. The waddling movements of the members of the Society, as they shakily made their way up the slope, reminded me, in a more subterranean way, of the scientists in radiation suits at my father's workplace. That both those children and those scientists now seemed so far away suggested political and industrial conditions had turned, or been misread, yet what was worth demolishing then had kept on, while the children and scientists had been asked to hang it up, although they would have been perfectly happy to continue doing what they were doing. This was not the kind of progress they imagined in those days.

My parents might have had some murky memories of us as babies, crying, remorseless, devouring engines of pain. Now we sat before them fully grown, ready, if we were lucky, to re-enact their lives, if poorly. My mother reminded my sister she would need help with her own newborn. If her husband had raised one before, it would all come back to him, but what was important was his attitude. She would come visit, of course, although that was not the same. They lived so far away, how long could she stay? 'It'd be nice to get even a little bit of help," my sister admitted. "We don't have a network out there, like you do here."

The back door opened into a gift shop, which used to be the servants' quarters. There were hiking maps for sale. I had no idea trails existed here, along with, perhaps, mountain lions. From the gift shop I retreated through a kitchen of wooden cabinets and yellow-tiled countertops, resembling those in un-renovated mid-century San Francisco homes like Ms. Hu's. I mentally noted colorful details which I would be called upon to recapture, such as samples of the author's microscopic handwriting and the teak "opium bed," a simple kang really, which the author and his wife slept on, a gift from Katherine Hepburn. The house otherwise possessed an inner austerity, the way its chambers were sealed off, which belied its relaxed exterior verandas. Windows seemed meant to see out only, all lined along the eastern side of the house, to catch the sunrise. The whole of it was a demon mask, something I thought to do with being buried in the middle of the century, on the edge of civilization. There were the sea-blue walls and ceiling, a profusion of mirrors, and minor touches of stagey vanity allowed by the couple, who after all were theater people, but otherwise the house was chaste. The masks in the foyer, despite "Chinese" touches, seemed out of place, for the ancients could not help, either. Some masks in museums feel eerily lifelike, but not these, as if the souls inhabiting them had been baffled by their journey and were wondering how long they were going to be stuck here. The most out-of-joint piece of furniture, though, was the player piano. Some kid, part of another tourist group that had just arrived, kept making it come alive.

There was a certain pressure living here to go outdoors, but it was exactly the heat in the interminable, oppressive afternoons that kept everyone inside. Personally I did not mind staying in. The heat gave me an excuse not to respond to anybody. Spring's colors leached away. At the same time, after wetter winters, the yellowed grass took on a glossier shine. The houses, in their unadventurous palette, did not stand out from the land, which became an extension of the watercolor by Ms. Hu hanging on the foyer wall, with its irregularly blurred and fine brushstrokes. The frame cost my father three hundred dollars. After the rains, the hills, outside, not those in the painting, turned green, while the painting stayed yellow. Ms. Hu, the painter, was now talking to my father on the phone. She wanted me to write something for the Society's literary journal. I told my father I did not write in Chinese. "In English," my father replied. "She wants you to write something about an American writer, so it should be in English."

It was built in clear lines, meant to let sun and air flow through, but they did everything they could to fight this. This was the influence of the wife. She confounded the classical design of a Monterey house with some notion of Spanish gloom. The oddities had been packed away upstairs. The bedroom, with a separate room for her, containing her jewelry and the so-called opium bed, featured a walk-in closet, while the study could only be gotten to through the closet. Inside were not one, but two desks, one for mundane correspondence, the other for the sacred work. A tight fit. A park ranger explained the author had given explicit instructions to his wife and servants that he was not to be disturbed whenever the door was closed. It seemed like a lot to go through just to write. Everything was shrunk down, become more obsessed, the handwriting, the model ships in bottles on the desk, the small window, like a porthole. To come all this way and build a mausoleum facing the mountain and the sun, only to spend your daylight hours cut off from them, for what? It was the monomania of the time. Somehow they had convinced themselves that if they thought hard enough, they could break through to the sublime. Had not my father been the same way? Meanwhile, had not the ancients always seemed to have composed lazily, in open air?

When I was ten, our house was broken into, and the thief thought to take my baseball-card and comic-book collections. I recited exactly what was lost to the police, having committed the collections' contents to memory, not just which players and years, but values based on official price guides. Then I did the same for the comics, which I never really read; I just kept them in plastic bags with backing boards to maintain their shape. The mind of this child would have burrowed into that bedroom and stayed sealed up there forever. I did go out running in the mornings, along the old railroad track, sometimes pumped the basketball back to life and wandered around in the park behind the house. I was not a stressed-out kid, more like the opposite. I had always thought it important to keep a clear mind, so that, in doing so, for example during exams, I remained calm, and the answers swam up before me. My sister was the opposite. For her performances, as my father recounted in his prose, she would get herself worked up into a nauseous state, then somehow overcome it, turning that tension into a strange beauty through a largely technical process. The winding and the release: I imagined she had not changed much.

I went downstairs through the living room, going against the suggested direction. The house was not furnished as in pictures in the brochure, taken with the author and wife. They probably did not watch TV. From the leftover scraps of stage furniture, I imagined how the couple might have whiled away an evening in quiet conversation or reading a book.

My sister did not bring anything except another CD. I thought about putting it on, but was afraid it might annoy my mother. Instead I shelved it where my father kept the others, along with dusty author copies of his book. The unplayed music resonated beside the unread memoir of the childhood of the woman who played the music.

The first time I entered this room, I had mistaken them for scrolls of vertically oriented landscapes, hung on either side of the fireplace. This time through, though, I noticed they were actually murals painted onto the walls themselves, done in pastels, only meant to emulate watercolor and evoke an oriental world. It was the same tack taken by Castiglione, whose mountains and swirling clouds flowed by willows and misshapen rocks. I reflexively imagined they were modeled on a Chinese original, but on closer look I found they were de-pictions of something I had never seen in a painting before, save for the one by Ms. Hu hanging in my childhood home: the same mountain and valley, bereft of houses and swimming pools, which few had ever found worth contemplating for the purposes of art, the view I had just seen outside this house.

{7}

My father requested de Bériot's "Scène de Ballet," which came as no surprise. It was one of a handful of pieces he asked my sister to play whenever she came home. All of these were works she had learned by the time she was twelve; there must have been a moment around then she became a musician in his mind, when he heard something resembling the records he listened to and that justified why he sat for those practices, which he would go on to do every day, until she attended college. She was obliging as always, even playing from memory, although it struck me she was probably called upon for these showpieces with great regularity, so memorization was not just for my father's sake; however, I did not think she played well the last few times I heard it. I say that respectfully as a nonmusician and, worse, as someone unaccustomed to listening to serious music. But I had heard her sound in the house all through my childhood: the stereotype lay imprinted in my head and, even if I could not analyze it, I could tell when it did not correspond to the execution. Of course she had matured, and presumably improved, and this was such an overfamiliar piece that any interpretation off the well-trod path would jar. For this time, though, the hoped-for effervescence was there, yet neither was it predictable, as if she had found a way to impose her own childlike sensibilities onto the piece, making its sweetness her own. How much of that, I could not help but think, had to do with her pregnancy and a sense of new beginnings?

There should have been an accompaniment, but she played it solo, not being the type of musician, I imagined, to utilize recordings, although I already knew this not quite to be the case, as I had listened to CDs of her with electronic loops. That absence of a second part shamed me, amplified by her choice of location, which was in front of the unoccupied upright piano in my parents' living room. If I had been asked, I would have correctly pointed out the piano needed tuning, but no one asked anymore. The last time I could keep up with her was when we had been children. Once I abandoned any pretense at musicianship, if I ever had it, my life began. My body had been nothing but a crude mechanism to transpose the notes on the page into the pressing of a key, for I did not hear them the way my sister did, in the ebb and flow that comprised musical phrasing; for me, it had always been about the isolate notes, flickering into existence at their appointed moments in time. The harmonic structure upon which they hung remained unknown to me.

In other words, in our family, my sister and father were the artists. My mother and I were the philistines. Like myself, my mother saw the world as atomized, as if the only way she could grasp it was to parse it into fragments. When she spoke, you could feel the force, in her teeth and tongue, biting the sentences apart. She held my sister's music under suspicion, which was ironic, since she was the one who came up with the idea to have her play violin, so her two children could perform duets. This turned out to be just a passing thought, however, and when I proved less than diligent, she seemed somehow relieved, while my sister's dedication grated on her over the years. As for where my father stood in all this, it was better to let him speak for himself. As he liked to remind you, he had written a book on the subject.

Not long after my sister's performance, my parents went to bed. She had been about to do the same, but the music had roused the baby, which meant she would have a hard time falling asleep. Instead we sat at the dining table and talked about how our father was dealing with retirement. If her concern was that he was bored, I reassured her that was not the case. So far he had been unsuccessful foisting leadership of the Society back onto Ms. Hu, and those activities, particularly the editing of the monthly newsletter, had been consuming his days since his last one at work. In addition, he had been advising Margaret, Rafael's widow, on the operation of her new business. My sister wondered what he knew about running a prepress, but she answered her own doubts; it was less about knowledge than the air of reliability everyone expected from him. He was a pillar in that little world of theirs, she observed, with an air of mockery. If that was why he was being brought in, then it was quite likely Margaret would hire him on as the new general manager.

Every time she was about to bring up the suggestion to my parents that they temporarily move in with her, my mother, as if sensing what was coming, cut her off or changed the topic in some way. Whether it was over her decision to pursue music as a field of study, her marriage, her move to the Midwest, or innumerable other resentments that had been, at least to me, lost to time, the barely concealed sleights between the two of them no longer could be traced to a discernible source. My own theory was it had to do with my sister's agelessness, which I now realized also had something to do with my mother's, for as my sister remained arrested at thirteen years old, my mother remained in her late thirties, and therefore nothing could be resolved. Would my sister's giving birth change that, so that both of them, along with her child, entered the stream of time? It was too early to tell. As for my father and myself, we had matured along the usual pathways, to a predictable outcome.

In reference to her earlier comment that evening during dinner, I said she probably did not know where to look for authentic Chinese food. It was no longer the Midwest of our youth; some of the states with the fastest growing Asian populations were now there, and taking into account the overseas Chinese students temporarily residing in university towns alone, a robust network had probably been established to keep them supplied with every amenity from their homeland.

Raising children in a culture that one did not grow up in presents challenges, as everybody knows, although what exactly those might be no one ever specifies. The burden assumed, I think, is the loss of accumulated generational wisdom, the cutting of the cord, so to speak, from one's ancestors. Of this there is no doubt, as my wife and I resorted to Dr. Spock for the most part, but, in retrospect, I think the value of such hand-me-downs may

Restaurants appealing to palates that were demanding to a degree unknown to us had no doubt appeared in the unlikeliest places. For someone monolingual like herself, these businesses might be hard to find, because their signage and advertising were only in Chinese; they had no need or inclination to derive income from the natives. She took this last comment as a dig at her lack of fluency in our parents' first language and countered by pointing out that she was the one who lived there, while I had never bothered to visit her.

It was typical of me to make such an assumption from my unnecessarily parochial point of view, she said. Our

be overblown. It strikes me that the principles of child-rearing are universal, which may be gleaned from a guidebook written by a contemporary American pediatrician as well as anything passed down by venerable Chinese mothers, and that human beings, especially their young, are an adaptable lot.

What feels missing lies at the other end of the generational spectrum, a sense of bewilderment when I look at my child's peers. I do not like to pronounce judgment on things I do not understand, but it is hard to escape the sense that these American children are being raised poorly; furthermore, it seems not just the parents' fault, but the culture's. Without trustworthy social mores, one tries to narrow down the range of comparison, but Chinese children simply do not exist on this side of the world. American society hides them from view, and at best they exist as grotesque stereotypes. I have spent some time establishing this background, because it seems I have been guilty, too, of perpetuating those stereotypes, or at least one of them, that parents she could understand, but it had always perplexed her why I, a second-generation like herself, should take on the often confused and incorrect standpoint of an immigrant. Did I have no interest in living in the country we were born and had grown up in? Was I entirely satisfied to reside in a terrarium our parents had constructed for us and themselves, a gauche memory of a homeland that no longer existed? It puzzled her because she had spent her entire childhood trying to escape that stranglehold. She had gone on to construct her own life. It had not been easy, but it had been eye-opening, whereas for myself . . . Circling back to the topic of our father's retirement, she found it

of the gifted Asian child who plays classical music; if I am, I have done so unconsciously and because I had few other welcome avenues.

These thoughts occurred to me one night as I was about to get ready for bed, when I heard a familiar tune floating gently down the hall. At first I took it for the stereo, but I came to recognize the quality of the sound, which was not that of Pinchas Zukerman or Kyung-Wha Chung, but strangely the sound I had come to know so well from sitting daily at my daughter's practices. Somehow, though, it was transformed. I had heard her play Mozart before, of course, and what she was doing then I never quite ascertained, but what I immediately began to reflect on was the effect her playing had on myself: my daughter was playing Mozart. It seems so flat and matter-of-fact to pronounce that now, but to hear her was to enter a universal flow that all of us had, until then, only glimpsed from a distance. It had been a matter of course for my wife and me to experience our lives apart from

extreme that I would step in for him and go on that road trip with Yvonne. It was none of my business to face his peers—Yvonne, Helen, Victor, Maisie, and Lincoln—and talk about Rafael, as if he were my friend. it, and from what I saw of our son, I did not think he would enter it either, but those sounds placed my daughter there. As I entered the room, I saw her against the backdrop of the living-room window, where behind her rose the image of the yellow Autumn Festival moon.[10]

I did not reply, realizing it was mostly her own fatigue talking now, but silently I made my own justifications, noting it was precisely to observe the country that I went, in ways she could not, perhaps because I saw it with the eyes of someone new, not just as our parents or Yvonne, but as Lena Wu. Other than that, I had been doing our father a favor. That was all. But she went on to say I was no longer a child, that I had my own life to lead, but it seemed as I grew older, I was becoming more and more embroiled in our parents' peculiar court intrigues. She said these things not out of spite but concern, so that I too could step out of that cage. Again I said nothing, but I felt she was wrong. I did not think theirs was a narrow world. It was far more layered than she gave it credit for, precisely because it was imaginary. There was more to it than the barren plains she had relocated to. I did not think I had dedicated myself to it, as she accused me of doing, but there was enough there to keep my interest, which was more than I could say for most of what people thought of as America.

---

[10] From *My Daughter the Prodigy* (Wǒ de tiāncái nǚ'ér) by Shih Ti-fu ("Steve").

{8}

WITH THE NEW JOB PREDICTABLY TAKING UP too much of his time, my father had to give up some of his Society duties, if not all of them. Ms. Hu would hear nothing of the latter, but she perked up when he suggested I take over the editing of the monthly newsletter. Of course I was neither the most qualified nor the most ardent to apply, but as Ms. Hu put it, if not in these words, who better in this day and age to edit the Society's communiqué than someone who neither wrote in Chinese nor was very interested in literature? The new members of the Society, it must be said, fit this profile better than the dour literati of bygone years. What we had now were men and women with an interest in personalized forms of writing, who treated it no differently than, say, a gym routine, that is, neither as dedicated writers nor scholars, but as ordinary people with only tangential experience to literature as an institution.

The task of the newsletter was to keep the Society front of mind, given how hard it was to gather all its members now, yet at the same time it needed to be a light read: at most it might carry a cultural feature, maybe a book review or two, the upcoming calendar, and summaries of events the Society had sponsored or participated in, so those who had not attended could still feel as if they had. My first editorial decision was to economize the format, reducing the ungainly saddle-stitched booklets my father manufactured to a folded eleven-by-seventeen-inch sheet, printed on both sides. I could now handle the xeroxing myself, and the single sheets could be handed out as calling cards. Down the road we should think electronically, perhaps even look into setting up a website, but because Ms. Hu had neither email nor an internet connection, she thought most of the members did not either.

With physical production thus simplified, most of the work involved layout, a process I hesitated to characterize as either design or editing, since it was hybrid: words poured into boxes, boxes resized to fit on the page, like puzzle pieces. If I made a box smaller, the words spilled out, so I would have to snip off the loose string of characters and slip them into another box, making sure the sense-connection to the preceding text was not lost. This must have been similar to what my father and Rafael once did with scissors and rubber cement: in other words, it was a game, with sufficient proximity and just enough distance from artistic creation. One did not read the words, not in a normal sense; they were a mix of image and language closer to calligraphy, with the sensation of the ghost coming up with the poem while one held the brush that glided across the paper. Once the pages were printed, copied, and folded, that earlier sense of fluidity and possibility was lost, and one was left only with the artifact.

No sooner had I told Ms. Hu of my plans for the one-sheet newsletter, a move she supported, then she got ideas for reviving the Society's journal. From the time of its inception, this was the Society's official periodical, its raison d'être. She brought out a pile of back issues, some of them dating back to her days in Shanghai. It had always been released irregularly, but the current running gap of three years between publications had been the longest since the Society's migration. Beyond the editorial task of assembling a collection of authors on a regular basis, I could see there would be production challenges, as she wanted to revive the values of the early editions, with their high-quality paper and binding. Standards had slipped in recent times—thin, yellow pages; amateur typography; poorly glued, cracking spines—but even these seemed beyond my capability and budget. One thing I thought I could improve was the kerning, which had not been updated from the first issue, the words on the page set in cramped, suffocating columns that seemed reflective of the humorlessness of the contributors and the sealed libraries where their books were shelved. Their resuscitation was her fixation, but I was open about my doubts. Allow me a few issues of the newsletter, I pleaded, then we'll talk.

It dawned on me what my father intended by sending me to her in the first place. He had not given me instructions on how to fight back then; rather, since it had been just the initial volley, my task was to set things up for the next time the topic was brought up, perhaps by myself again, or somebody else, so that she might take it more seriously. This was how to get these older folks to bend, for they did everything on principle. What, I wondered, had it taken to get the generation after them to think in terms of expedience? She was old, older than my father by a generation. In a Chinese timeline, the gap between the two of them was exactly when their world, the center of the universe, fell to pieces. Now all that was left could be found at the coordinates of her house, the only section of this city laid out on a predictable grid: north-south numbered, east-west alphabetical. Where else would it be found, if not there, where all the lost Chinas had ended up? But Ms. Hu in particular seemed not to be of that neighborhood, corner, or block. Stepping into her presence seemed like stepping into an era all parties had since agreed to forget. She alone was the Society, a testament to its survival through a century of disaster and exile: Shanghai, Hong Kong, Taipei, and finally, anticlimactically, here. It had seen better days; when the Society crossed the ocean, there had been a less dispersed émigré colony, so a kind of renaissance took place, but now it consisted only of occasional lunches, juried watercolor shows, dance performances, scholarship award ceremonies, and, especially, student poetry-recitation contests. The children who recited Li Po without comprehending him at the time might receive a spark of enlightenment much later in their lives, and for that it was still worth it, but these events were, to be honest, more vital to the Society than the other way around.

The sound of rain echoed in the school's unheated halls. In the classroom I entered, carrying a paper shopping bag filled with newsletters, which weighed as heavily as rocks, parents filled the middle rows, some of them looking as if they may as well be back in China, with the grave air they projected and pink jackets and scarves they wore; others, though, could have come from any other public school in the district. The front rows consisted of the contestants, selected or volunteered from around the city, in their dressy best. To the side sat the teachers, looking the most relaxed of anybody. They were the judges. All of them, I could tell, regarded this as just another school activity, which it was and which was good: to pass this wisdom on not just to future generations but beyond the traditional boundaries of the culture itself was the goal.

I counted off a short stack of newsletters, enough for every parent in the classroom by my rough guess, left them on a chair by the doorway, then found a seat in the last row. The tall windows that ran down one side and reached up almost to the ceiling did a poor job of insulation, the panels at eye level were frosted, and one of the windows by the ceiling corner could not be shut, which let in a draft. The teachers did not bother with the room lights. The rain viewed in the upper window frames began falling harder, drumming against the glass. Outside, kids continued shooting baskets in the downpour, bouncing their ball between parked cars and barely avoiding hitting a hood or windshield. The texture of the air here by the ocean felt thinner, more metallic and vegetal.

One anxious boy in a green sweater vest stood in the clearing in front of the room and recited Wang Zhihuan's famous quatrain with a swallowed enunciation indifferent to any meanings he may have gleaned from the poem. This was a work I imagined my father and Yvonne probably knew by heart. Its effect hinged, like much of the Tang, on perspectival shifts. Perhaps because they were not conditioned by photography and cinema, its poets made a technique of those moments, from mountaintop or country under siege to the detail of a single, graying hair. Wang's was not that kind of a tour de force; rather, the shift was telegraphed prosaically and unsurprisingly. It did have the advantage of musicality and naturalness, making it suitable for children. Not that any of this registered on the boy. Simply understanding what was happening was the most he could pull from it, and even that was only the barest glimmer in his mind: something about going up the stairs. That was how I once took in the poem too, while the words, and their rhythm, having been pressed into my memory as sound, bloomed much later with its latent wisdom. They would do the same for that boy.

More reciters followed, a parade of towers, moons, lakes, rivers, mountains, sky, clouds, rain, snow, mist, blossoms, and birds. These images were alien to the children who were speaking them, if they understood them at all, for the fog they knew, which came in the summer, was not an evocative suggestion of absence so much as a force of nature that wiped out everything in its path. As for mountains and lakes, most of them had probably never even been to Tahoe or Yosemite, but it was clear, from everything I had ever observed, it was not important whether they understood what they were saying or not. They were good kids. They took the contest seriously. There was something, probably the expressions of their parents and teachers as they faced down the poem, that made them take it seriously. In this exercise, modest after all, they were making a civilization. It was an old method. I thought of the billions spent at the lab my father once worked for to build lasers and atom smashers that would ring through the ages, but the fine sentiments being repeated here, fixed to a character-writing system beginning to fade after millennia, would probably last longer. Right now our hearts trusted science, but it was good to hedge our bets. It may come down to a broken-down classroom full of kids and the discouraged adults pushing them through their paces who might one day have to stand in for humanity. What they had already committed to memory seemed to have as good a chance of lasting as anything.

Once the recitals were over, I stepped into the hallway, where I bumped into Ms. Hu. She complained of the weather, which was making her bones ache, and led me to wonder why she continued to live in the fogbound outer avenues. I encouraged her to at least spend more time outside city limits, as we had in Danville, and that the audience for this sort of thing had long since moved out to the suburbs. Chinatown was nothing but a symbol now and no longer a hub for meaningful cultural activity. She acknowledged as much, but pointed out she was too old to move and that there was still enough activity in the city to keep her preoccupied, so she would see out the remainder of her time here. Despite her aches and pains, she was in good spirits because she had received the first issue of the newsletter under my editorship and had seen the lead feature by Yvonne Fung, an excerpt from the introduction to her new book. What an auspicious debut for me, she said, reeling in the most exciting contributor to the newsletter in years. I did not tell her that Yvonne had been the *only* person I could think of to write something, but I did mention my trepidations over not doing the Society justice, failing to live up to its history.

The history, she said, was always going to be there. She spoke as one who had made it. The past would take care of itself.

It was the future she was worried about. I should just keep moving forward, as we were doing here, with these children.

I felt I had the wherewithal for the task, just not . . . what was it? The temperament? Or desire? Were such things required to schedule, manage budgets, get people to contribute, and speak and write on the Society's behalf? I did not have the heart to tell her that I found Yvonne's introduction rather disappointing.

She moved into a large room off the hall. This would be one of her increasingly rare public appearances. Regardless of the damp and cold, she still had the energy to work as she always had, one more, although perhaps the last, in an intolerable line of dilettante-scholars dating back to, so it was said, the Sung Dynasty. Her watercolor was the centerpiece, taking up an entire wall. It was strange to think I had seen it when I visited her in her mildewy living room, when it had been lying on top of a table, not as it was now, transformed by this makeshift gallery. The multipurpose room was not well lit enough to properly display it, not for work of this type, made of nuance and negative space. For example, the light and shadow at play on the paper could be mistaken for brushstrokes, but under these conditions that sort of subtlety was too fine. The correct place for it would be a pavilion overlooking a pond and garden, fooling you into thinking it was the view. But did she care where her work was hung now or, for that matter, in what setting it was produced? This was no art gallery. It was a pit stop, and she would do what she could in what was not really a studio. But then it was no different a thousand years ago. After all, she, like her predecessors, was not painting from life: those mountains, gorges, and rivers did not lie outside her window. The window in her head looked upon a world alien to this one, one that really existed and perhaps still did to this day, if barely. She had not been there since childhood. How did she do it? I thought of something my father once said about how the classical artists did not paint from nature; their practice was based on what was seen in the mind's eye and what might exist in correspondence to it. In other words, they were poets. So could such an imagination subsist anywhere? I asked him. No, he replied, not when it goes up against something too foreign to it.

I dropped copies of the newsletter onto the folding table by the entrance. The thoughts captured on those sheets of paper were now likewise, in their less accomplished way, set free. I did not anticipate there to be many takers, but as the rain cleared and the sunlight glittered off the wet metal of the cars in the lot, people began to wander in, looking for a place to rest their feet, and mindlessly picked up copies of the newsletter, thinking it a program or just to use as a fan. It was not clear to them what the paintings on the wall were for or what was the point of the sheet of paper in their hands. Someone would carry on after me, just as I picked up where my father left off. That was what kept it going. You did what you could, and somebody else took over.

She sat down at a pair of children's tables that had been pushed together, covered by strips of parchment. In front of her was an inkstone and brush. Once she took brush to paper, a change took place. She worked in fluid, corkscrew turns of the wrist, bursts of motion, strokes twisting off the surface of the page, then spiraling back down again. What came first: the thought or its expression? Of course Ms. Hu was not "think-ing" what she was writing. It was preselected, probably a line from an old poem. Most often that was the case, something already composed, but the illusion of the form was such that it seemed, particularly in running script, as if such thoughts were being spontaneously generated on paper. What it really was, was nothing but discipline.

"Good calligraphy is like a flock of birds darting from trees." Huai-su's drunken scroll, Su Dongpo's more state-ly script—actually written in his own hand! These had come down to us along with the precise language that had been wo-ven into them. The handscroll was almost a thousand years old. Never mind the writing itself, the moment had survived into this very one as we stood looking at it: a dense, dark line, the ink soaking into the ancient paper, because the calligrapher had pushed so hard into it that it leaked into the spaces in between, rendering some of the characters into illegible bricks. Maybe the brush tip did not leave the page. One could see up close the threads between one word and the next. They said your line speaks your fate. Su Dongpo's seemed heavy, burdened, yet strong enough to generate freedom of movement. Ms. Hu's, on the other hand, was almost not there. Unlike Dongpo, she had made her peace with the world, all the more remarkable, knowing what she had experienced. Who would you rather be?

Now it was my turn to get up in front of the crowd. I looked over the heads of the adults and children, into the up-per windows, where the rain had started up again. The kids squirmed around. My words floated up into the din ringing against the roof:

"I have to admit, when I was a kid, I didn't like reciting poems. I thought, what's the point of parroting these words you don't understand? I'm sure—from the looks on some of the faces I've seen today—some of you feel the same way. It seems like a form of punishment, doesn't it? An unusual one, a very Chinese one, you might say. But it isn't meant to be punishment. Or if it is, it's the kind that helps you remember. You might not understand the meaning of the poems you have been asked to recite today. Or you might understand the words, which in of itself is no mean feat, but you have not yet gained their wisdom. It's not a matter of being smart enough. What those old poets knew is something that takes years to understand. Even I haven't been around long enough to understand them fully. It takes time. That's their beauty. Because when you recite these poems, and get to know them by heart, you carry them inside you for the rest of your lives. They're there, waiting for you to catch up, and one day you will. It comes, maybe in a moment you weren't expecting. In a flash, in a sneaky way, you realize you've changed.

"So you see, you don't really have to know Chinese to recite Chinese poems. Rote memorization, which gets a bad rap nowadays, is another way of getting past the artificial barriers of language and culture. Another way is writing the poems, as we're doing today, with brush in hand, without truly understanding the words. To be honest, I've always been uncomfortable with those celebrations of being Chinese, as if it were an achievement in of itself. Some people think Chinese New Year is that celebration, but it isn't. It's something more important. Don't get me wrong. I'm proud of my heritage. It might just be me, but as good, bad, or indifferent it is to be Chinese, those celebrations seem to be drawing a line between myself and others. Today isn't one of those days. We celebrate Chinese poetry because it is there for everyone. If you recite these old poems, without even understanding the language, which is something anyone can do, you begin to partake of one of the great cultural patrimonies of the world, something that once only belonged to emperors and the extremely privileged, but now belongs to, well, just about everybody.

"I saw some serious faces out there today. Too serious, I think. We're here to have fun, make memories, and share. We're here to show traditional Chinese culture isn't something intimidating. That's my hope and that of the Society I represent. But I have to admit, there's a side of me that thinks, 'It's good to see fear in their eyes.' I'm not talking about stage fright. I'm not talking about our students, who are wonderful and diligent, but the parents and teachers. The adults sense, maybe not fully, I feel, that despite the lighthearted nature of what we're doing today, something lies beyond, something we will all face one day. The words are something you master, as you encounter adversity in life. They will in some cases be all you have. But they will be enough. Because you carry them with you. Read. Memorize. Recite to yourself in times of struggle. It gives you courage. Nobody knows why, but everybody finds this to be true."

{9}

I DID NOT LEARN OF THE SATELLITE OFFICE Rafael maintained in the Bay Area, in Belmont, to be exact, until my father asked me to meet him there. He wanted to introduce me to Rafael's widow. It was only then I understood something that I had previously only discerned dimly, about why Rafael's plant was located in Los Angeles, while he continued to reside with his family in Northern California. He had planned to relocate for a long time, my father would later explain to me, since he hated the drive back and forth, but Margaret disliked LA's climate, which she considered too hot, and its culture, which she considered vapid. As a result he was never able to make the move.

In fact my father had misremembered. It would not be the first time for me to meet her; I had once before, at Rafael's funeral, but that had only been a brief conferral of condolences, which I doubted she recalled. For me, perhaps because the deceased felt like a distant relative, the grief and atmosphere of shame only hovered likewise at a distance, in the stark Peninsula light, so I could observe with a clear line of sight. I recollected the wreaths set in the reception room, decorated with white strips written on in Chinese script, some by my father's steady hand, the altar suffused in smoke from sandalwood incense. There was Rafael and Margaret's strange son, carrying the urn at the front of a procession, in a clangor of bells and cymbals. Most vividly, I remember the startling image of bald monks in yellow robes, maybe four or five in all, emerging from a van onto the hot blacktop, under a cloudless blue sky.

Rafael had not been a Buddhist. Like my parents, he and Margaret probably possessed a hazy understanding of a world beyond ours, populated by ancestors and other beings, but it likely did not go much further than that. For Margaret, Buddhism was a close enough approximation to this, and that meant everything was going into the fire, a thought that made me uncomfortable on this hot, dry day, with the poisonous sun leaving all of us sweating in our dark suits. A burial in the verdant earth seemed a more welcome refuge. Anyway, if the deceased could convince himself to playact a murder, who knew what, in the end, he really believed in?

Memorial speeches were made against the backdrop of an automated slideshow; however, Margaret did not give one of them, which was understandable. To my surprise, their son did step up to the podium for a short speech, delivered, even more surprisingly, in anger at his father, for putting them in this predicament while ruining his own meticulously designed legacy. Revulsion rippled through the audience, the visceral response to witnessing someone to be pitied losing their emotional control, but for me, at first anyway, there was something about his performance that had me thinking he was in possession of his faculties, a hint of arrogance and sense of theatrics, as if the intention were to shock, so I came around to my second thought: he should not have done that.

However, after the speeches, but before the internment of the ashes, it seemed everyone had taken the young man's outburst in stride. In muted conversation on the outdoor patio, they agreed he was grieving and went out of their way to make excuses. My father dissented: "He doesn't understand. His father suffered too, but he can only think of himself." It seemed from the reactions of his friends they could not bring themselves to blame the boy. "At some point his mother's going to pass the business on to him," he went on. "That was the plan, but he's not in the right frame of mind for it." The topic of succession was not a priority, and instead the conversation thankfully turned to the familiar task of closing ranks.

The Belmont office was set amid the scent of juniper and sea fog, a tower in the woods. It was still weird to me that a five-minute drive from downtown was all it took to enter this sanctuary, but it was the same all around the Bay, developments spliced into forest or shoreline, as in a collage.

The interior of the lobby did not turn away from the environs it had been placed in and instead gave visual access to it, even as it was separated from it by the picture window that made up the lengthwise wall. This was, I appreciated, Rafael's first sight on arriving at work. He stared out from here, perhaps in a frantic moment of thought over sales or logistics, or alternatively, while dreaming of Wang Wei. Rafael was no longer here, but that was not the only reason why the offices felt desolate. Behind me, through another glass partition, were empty cubicles and dust-coated office equipment. It was not at all like the one in Monterey Park, with its industrious population that was the hub of a modest empire. Perhaps there had been a time he thought of moving the plant north, closer to family and home. Profits may have been flush then, and he may have been willing to take the operational fixed cost higher. These were things my father would take a closer look at. One thing was for sure, even to my layman's eye: they did not need this much space just to keep the files where Margaret's accountants and lawyers could conveniently get to them.

When was the last time she was here? She must have unlocked the doors for the police; I imagined the authorities would have wanted to examine the premises for evidence. Now, yes, they were cold and lonely, but in an off-kilter way, seemingly hardly used and worn out at the same time. The lobby walls seemed to have been left bare from the very beginning, as if the tiniest luxury were a distraction that could not be afforded. On the other side of the plexiglass, the blinds over a set of smaller windows were closed. I went ahead and turned them, to a view of the mist. I imagined Margaret at one of the empty meeting tables, looking at Rafael as he fed her details on the business, with a half-understanding look on her face. She did not need to know everything then, so long as enough assurances were made that the ramparts around their fortune would hold. In her marriage, I am guessing, she had been the quiet one. She was cut loose now, having lost her husband's initiating energies, and it would be up to my slow-to-burn father to resupply them.

Once he became aware I was outside, my father called me into the meeting room. Helen and Victor were already there, seated at a long rectangular table, along with an older woman two-thirds the size of Helen, whom I took to be Margaret, and an older man I took to be Uncle Rafael's ghost. The lack of anything decorative in the previous room, whether artistic or vegetal, drew all the more attention to the classical-style painting behind my father at the head of the table. It depicted a couple and their daughter under the roof of their house, with a pair of swallows swooping overhead, symbols of fidelity and domestic tranquility.

Without acknowledging my entrance, Helen continued to assure her audience, presumably Margaret, although I was not sure about the other man, that by the end Rafael actually had very little to do with the day-to-day. In fact he rarely came into the office anymore, so in a sense, little had changed. She did not mean this as a complaint, by the way. In fact, his absence should be taken as proof of his genius: the system he had built, its rigid set of procedures, proved able to run itself and even survive its creator's death. I did not know how much of an indiscretion it might be, at this late juncture, to mention all the time he spent away from the office. Presumably Helen knew what he was do-ing while ostensibly on business in LA. As Helen went on, I was able to pick up clues here and there as to the source of the tension in the room, namely Margaret's refusal to appoint Hel-en permanent general manager, although I did not think any of them noticed I was now aware of this. It seemed Margaret had granted Helen only interim status, while keeping the financial team close; the man I could not identify must have been the person who oversaw that department. She had taken the ini-tiative to move most of the financial files, still retained as paper archives, to Belmont. If Rafael did have any genius, it was in his foresight to remove any leverage Victor and Helen might have had far in advance of their ever needing it. They could threaten to leave, start their own competitor, and bring the staff with them, but they could not take his systems and machines. It was the people who were the most replaceable.

Margaret did not reply other than to indicate that she heard, although whether she agreed or not was another matter and unintelligible: she had not removed her green coat; her hair, which had been straight at the funeral, was now waved; and her figurative mask, which she put on to pass the time until she was ready to become whomever she was meant to become without her husband, never slipped.

With his characteristic certainty in pointing out the inconclusive, my father said that Margaret had not yet decided what to do; for now she had merely asked him to take a look around and provide a perspective. On the face of it, coming from him, the man being positioned to take Helen's place, this admission might come off as redolent with irony, if not as an outright threat. My impression was that Margaret did not yet understand the magnitude of her power. She was not running a representative government or even a very large company: she had the right to do as she pleased. There were rules, yes . . . but this was ownership. This was why they had you read the Confucian classics in your youth, my father might say, so when the time came, you would know how to act. Was Margaret acting properly?

My mother had warned my father not to poke his nose into the traps his sly old friend had left behind, but she knew it was too late and that the role he took in such situations was at any rate passive, as other people's business found him, not the other way around. What he provided, sanity and stability, were qualities, not outcomes, or rather, they were their own outcomes, if one desired them. God knew he had better things to do, favors he owed, but now in his retirement it seemed as if he had more work than ever. In Margaret's case, it would be a temporary job. She had received queries about the company, including one from an old business partner of Rafael's in Hong Kong. It was probably the solution she was looking for, since she had no long-term interest in ownership and was just hoping for a way to set her mind at ease while putting what happened behind her.

"We're not kids," Helen said. "We know it's the 'consultants' who take your job in the end."

My father insisted he was no businessperson.

"But we do trust your judgment," Margaret added as justification. "My husband did. He said you were the only one who saw things clearly."

"He's making fun of me, even now."

She explained he would work from this office, with Mike and Eileen. That was why she had the financial records moved. As they all got up for lunch, Helen finally noticed me, sitting in the corner.

"That's my son. Don't mind him. I asked him to come by to pick up something."

"So you've got him working for you too? Wait, I recognize you."

"Yes, we met before at the office in Monterey Park."

"You were with that writer, what's-her-name."

She asked how the research was going and when the story would come out. It was a book, not an article, I reminded her. The truth was that Yvonne had been vague about its publication, and I had the feeling I might only find out about it through my father or the Society grapevine. By the time the book was finally published, Helen pointed out, nobody would remember Rafael and the scandal. Although she did not seem to grasp the point, I mentioned this was by design, so its events could be received by its readers outside the news cycle, while I did not mention what perhaps only I suspected, that Rafael would not be its main character.

After I introduced myself to Margaret, who claimed to remember me from the funeral, although this may have just been courtesy, my father instructed me to stay behind with Mike. I was to check on a property in downtown San Francisco and let him know what I found there. He did not mention what I might expect or the purpose of this task, although I had an idea of both. With clockwork choreography, Mike went off into the cubicle maze just as my father led the others toward the elevators. The senior accountant invited me into what he explained was the old boss's executive suite. Using a key card, he opened the door and then gestured for me to get behind the desk into the chief's chair. I wondered if this was some kind of joke or comment on my father taking over the company. The sensation of sinking into the not-that-worn leather was a bit disappointing. No power flowed through me, nor any thrill of usurpation. If anything, I felt my power, or rather my energy, draining. I calculated the ways this act might be interpreted as a betrayal of the founder's memory, but I really was a neutral party in all this, with no stake in the awkward spectacle I had just witnessed.

I took the VP of finance to be my father's age. The expression of incredulity that had been fixed upon his leathery face since I had arrived, the face whose features themselves lay hidden behind a set of bulky eyeglass frames, was, I had begun to discern, simply its resting state, but it still made it hard to say anything to him without thinking one had given offense. He sat down on the other side of the desk, fired up a cigarette without asking permission, and proceeded to call Helen a total snake, which meant that Victor was somehow even worse; with her, at least, she was the one who did the talking. The old boss was better than them, of course, he said, looking around for an ashtray, but the fact alone that he tolerated them diminished him in everybody's eyes. He laughed weakly at this. It took me a moment to understand this was his stab at humor.

The deal with Hong Kong would fall through, he went on. I got the feeling it was rare for him to have an audience. It was hard enough to convince an investor to come in under the best circumstances, never mind these conditions. She should be looking for a local suitor, but was too trusting of this "old friend" of her husband's and had not made any calls. Now she had put all her eggs in one basket and was shocked when he told her that they would back off once they sensed her desperation. Is that what these businesspeople did? she said in an unguarded moment, nor did she understand how much it was to ask someone to make the whole mess disappear, as she was asking my father to do. He was a good man, Mike allowed, and he knew what he was getting into, which was to focus on layoffs. One thing that had to be taken care of right away, though, was to outsource the human-resources function, which currently belonged to Helen. That had been her original role, actually, before she got promoted, and even if she was not particularly good at it, it was an easy job in the company. The staff were plants basically, although for this task my father would need to hire an outside consultant, not only to take the heat, but to make sure they were in compliance with state and local regulatory statutes.

Heat? Would the staff really revolt, take it out on the organization? It was less a matter of internal politics than external perceptions, he replied. From dealing with the media during the scandal, he said, giving me a knowing look, they had learned it was important to protect the company's reputation, and specifically Margaret's. No, the staff themselves were not like that, most of them had been with the company a long time, and the old boss had brought them up, in effect. They were right to think something bad was happening, but what could they do about it? Even he had stuck it out with the company all these years, having been with it from the beginning, which was why he had ended up with this absurd title. He was sure he was in over his head, and to tell the truth by the end he hated the old man too. It was understandable, was it not, if he felt trapped, dependent, and resentful? Now he was the only person in the organization Margaret trusted. A longtime employee like himself knew his boss in a different way than others did. The relationship between them was closer than friendship, since they saw each other every day, in closest proximity, with all the implications of education and control. At the same time it was all only through the prism of business. Human emotions drifted in and out of the picture, with no impact, but through the numbers he saw Rafael in an odd way, a kind of inner self only an accountant would know.

I told him a recent story I read about a privatized factory in China that laid off hundreds of workers. The workers got together after hours, cornered their boss in his office, locked the doors, and beat him to death with hammers.

"You think that's how we treat people?"

I told him I did not care how the company treated its staff. I was just concerned for my father.

What were the chances of Margaret finding another buyer? If my father was going to oversee any transition, it seemed most likely it would be the one to her son. Yes, that had been the original plan, Mike admitted, but things were different now, and she could not wait for him to grow up. Furthermore, he added, the real reason for the tension in that meeting was due to the relationship between the boy and Victor. The two of them had grown close over the years. Of course that was entirely thanks to Victor, who had been planting seeds from the day the boy was born. The mother had tried coming between them ever since the incident, but it was not clear how successful she had been. It occurred to me now that this may have explained the son's outburst at the funeral, and with Yvonne's theory in mind, I tried seeing through Mike's biases as well: What if, for all their faults, Helen and Victor had the best interests of the company at heart? Maybe they were running things the way the old man would have wanted, and he was the one who wanted his son to follow Victor's lead. As long as they received their rewards and nice titles, it seemed to me they would not have a problem with turning the company over to the proper heir when the time came.

At that moment, a mousy-looking young woman entered, cradling a laptop in one hand. I assumed this was Eileen. As she sat down, she did not lift her head from the screen. The room slid into silence, except for the sound of her typing.

"I adjusted it last night," she told Mike, still without looking up.

"The unit in San Francisco?"

"Yes. It wasn't entered correctly in the books."

He turned to me. "You're already doing good work. Keep it up." He reached into the desk, pulled out a set of card keys, and slid it over to me. "I checked already, so no need to waste your time. We'll probably just end up selling it."

I would not have guessed my father would be behind the wheel again so soon, much less commuting to a new job, but here I was, imagining the route he would be taking: some nights, depending on whim or traffic, he would take the San Mateo Bridge, but most of the time he would probably climb toward the city: around the Burlingame bend, past its seedy hotels and car dealerships; down the Brisbane causeway, where the glass-and-concrete office parks parted enough to provide a view of the sun-dappled bay behind them; and then to merge into the traffic crawling onto the Bay Bridge, stuck on a skyway stranded midflight over scrap-metal yards and contractor-supply showrooms.

In summer, the fog was a rolling mountain face, wiping the city away on a scale that was difficult to comprehend, even as one saw it happening, but in winter, it was gentler, sitting over it like a translucent dome. Instead of following traffic onto the bridge, as I was imagining my commuting father would, I took the last exit to San Francisco. The sky, still smeared red, dropped from view as I arrived at street level. Cars and bikes danced around each other, past murals, palm trees, and bell towers of baroque churches, wrapped, almost warmly, in mist. The air smelled of brine. I cut through one-way streets and block-long connector alleys with practiced familiarity until popping back out onto the main thruway headed downtown. The address was a condo at the end of a cul-de-sac. It looked renovated, at odds with the old brick warehouses, or what used to be old warehouses, that took up the rest of the block. I rode the elevator to the third floor and found myself in a long, over-lit corridor in what resembled a dormitory. Everything felt thin and poorly constructed, but this seemed to be the preferred style these days.

The key worked. I thought of house-hunters, Yvonne's clients, barging with impunity into other people's homes, drunk on hope. This was not me; I was working on behalf of the landlord. I wondered if this unit had ever been put on the market. It was possible no one else but myself, my father, Mike, and Eileen even knew it existed. Oh, and whoever was living here. My first impression was of the dark wood molding on the walls, with cabinetry and furniture to match. No plants. It seemed monkish and solid, too serious, with an unambiguous masculine tone. It may have served as a retreat for an older man, someone who had already settled elsewhere, yet it was no love nest. I glided my hand along the walls and windows, not looking at anything in particular, not observing it the way a buyer or writer might. I did not take pictures; I would remember it well enough to convey what my father needed to know. When had someone last been here? The water and electricity were still running. An empty beer can was still in the trash, a half-drunk bottle of chardonnay in the fridge. I could imagine a young woman, sitting on the couch in the dark right now, thinking I was a ghost. I pulled the shade, letting the dying light of the bay flow in, diffusing her dream-image.

For some reason I saw her as the caricature of a Puritan, severe looking, wearing a black coat, pants, and shoes. It would be better just to come out with it and ask her all my father wanted to know. He got himself killed because of you. How did you live with this burden? What made you think you could run from it? Was it all about money, and if so, how much did you take?

{10}

WHEN YVONNE SENT ME THE INTRODUCTION, she let me know the novel had been completed as well, but professed ignorance of its publication date. The publisher lacked the funds to pay for the print run, although their positive cash flow was not, she assured me, the development keeping her in suspense. If it were, she mentioned matter-of-factly, the book would never see the light of day; rather, she was going to put the money up herself, but was waiting for her latest real estate deal to close and along with it the receipt of her commission. At this point the novel was a pure vanity project. She did not expect to make her investment back from sales, but rather than a disappointment, it sounded as if this kind of thing was to her more the rule than the exception, a simple reality of literary economics.

Given the book's publication was of incidental interest even to its author, the completion of an obligation whose costs had run over, I was not surprised to find out about it not from her but on a TV talk show being shown on the local Chinese-language channel. Yvonne was there being interviewed by the host, a long-time local news fixture and someone I had met once at a Society event and glimpsed another time shopping at the nearby Costco. They were in a black-box studio, presumably not more than ten miles from where I was watching the simulcast, swiveling in office chairs against a backdrop of houseplants and bird-and-flower embroidery. When the host asked her how she came up with the story, it occurred to me that Rafael's accidental, self-inflicted death, the biggest community scandal of my lifetime, had already been wiped clean from the collective memory bank. This was, as I have mentioned, not unexpected, and Yvonne sounded prepared to rehash. The riveted host nodded as if he were hearing all this for the first time, which I knew he was not, since he had sedulously reported the case only a little over a year ago.

"The novel's not really at all about the alleged murder attempt."

"You say *alleged*. Didn't he bring a gun with him? His intentions were very clear, weren't they?"

"Well, no. The police report distinctly states he was only looking to put a scare into the guy."

"But if he was just looking to scare him, why was the gun loaded?"

"We don't know if he knew it was loaded at the time. Of course we now know that it was. He found out too, right?"

They never got around to the substance of the novel itself, or very much about the novel at all. I noticed she was wearing a new pair of glasses, stylishly wide frames with thin, gold rims and tinted lenses.

The next day, while running an errand for my father, I stopped at a Chinese bookstore in Milpitas. At first I thought they did not have Yvonne's book, since it was not on the new-release display table at the front of the store, but then I found it shelved in the stacks, spine out, as if it were already of secondary interest. A quick examination proved it had been digitally printed, on too-white paper, the modern equivalent of the yellowy pocket paperbacks of my youth, except where in the past the cheapness of the quality owed to overproduction, now it owed to the reverse, scarcity or, if you preferred, lack of demand. Perhaps it was that sheen on the paper that lent these productions their ersatz quality, but they seemed less like books than printouts. I bought it and stepped out into the warm South Bay evening, onto a crowded strip-mall sidewalk, and waited in line at a popular Jiangnan restaurant. A seat opened at the bar, with a view of a young man pulling noodles by hand, and I ordered a Shanghai-style rice with salted pork and greens. On the overhead television was Yvonne, in a rerun of the same show I had just seen the day before.

It was an indefatigable reminder that she had neglected to let me know of her book's publication, even though I was, as far as I knew, the only editor to run an excerpt from it. To get back in touch, I thought I could ask her for a review or column, a bit of self-promotion she would probably agree to, given she was now doing the local talk show circuit. For a review, there was already a growing pile on my desk of self-published memoirs and cookbooks forwarded to me by Ms. Hu that she could choose from. For an op-ed or sǎnwén, loose thoughts, there was no shortage of noncontroversial subjects I could ask her to comment on, although the subject of the local housing market, always a hot topic among Society members, seemed the best fit for her. Ms. Hu would probably remind me to keep things literary, though.

My father used to complain that he found it impossible to read Western books one-handed, whereas the ingenuity of the traditional Chinese book lay in its total design as an object: vertical text, read in columns running right to left, printed on thin and flexible paper. It was a civilized way to read: with my left hand, I folded the verso half of Yvonne's novel backward and used my left thumb to pull the recto page in, revealing one line at a time of the page behind it as I read, the vertical edge acting as a ruler, all the while handling my chopsticks with my right.

The book began in medias res with Rafael's murder attempt or, rather, his attempt to put a scare into his rival. From there, it leapt back in time, abruptly, to the beginning of the story, before setting forth again along the highways I had driven with Yvonne, heading north to south. I read quickly, skimming the parts I already knew about from personal experience while looking for those I did not. It was a disorienting quest, because Yvonne did not write in strict chronological order and instead broke up time to her liking, but eventually I got to what I was looking for, which was what Lena did after she left LA. This then led to the next question: How did Yvonne find out?

Without much transition, Lena appeared in a city that resembled Sacramento, with a new occupation, running a private bus line first from San Francisco, then from Auburn. This was not where I had thought to find her, and as for the business, how did she get it going? Frustratingly, the author had provided scant detail of how she arrived and established a venture only a few months after the incident with Rafael; although in regards to the latter, there was a hint that the money may have come from what my father had suspected all along lay at the heart of the matter. Yvonne seemed to have come to the same conclusion: Rafael's act could not have been a crime of passion, because he was not, by nature, passionate. Was this my father's influence or had she uncovered new information since our trip together? I would have to ask her. Nor could I ignore the possibility that the passage may have been nothing but a fiction, designed for its dramatic impact or, as unlikely a consideration it may have been in this case, market appeal. Other aspects felt off, for reasons that I could not quite pinpoint, most significant among them her portrayal of Rafael. How much more did she know about him, and what had she found out? Like much of the novel itself, I could not tell which of these qualities were due to insights from newfound evidence and which to the shortcomings of a fabrication that nonetheless managed, in its writerly attention to detail, to achieve verisimilitude.

For that was the thing about Yvonne's prose: I could see each scene as if it were being played out before me. There was a moment, as I tried to pry meat from bone with my teeth, that the vinegary sauce from the sweet-and-sour ribs I had just ordered splattered across the page, flinging edible ink over the words printed there. Remember that in Chinese one stray stroke or mark can completely change the meaning. Perhaps it was due to this reinscription, but the bustling, fragrant restaurant I was sitting in became the atmosphere of the scene I happened to be reading. For a moment I lost sight of both where I was and where *she* was. The rubbery nib sprang from my mouth onto the table and bounced upward along a trajectory that I turned my head to follow: to the overhead fluorescent lamp fixtures and the altar tucked into a corner of the ceiling, where a copper pot stuffed with joss sticks glinted in the artificial light.

She sat at the window, watching the fractured sun caught in chips of chrome and glass, the spinning balls and blinking neon taking on richer hue and clearer outline as the sky darkened. The tall buildings were all hotels. The grid, beginning to glow, might have gone on forever in one direction, for the desert would not have impeded it. Mountains would, in another direction, in the form of the Geiger Grade. Eventually a plane appeared, descending out of the sky, flying lower than the mountain peaks, skimming over the valley floor. She took her time. She had seen this view before, more often facing the opposite direction, so she would be looking at the Sierras, dwarfing everything in the window frame and seeming impenetrable, even though she would have just driven across them without any great effort. She had been to this town before too, and plenty just like it, but it did not occur to her until now it was a wasteland, in some sense a sacred place. If she were in Asia, this would be Lhasa, rising out of the arid plateau, on a chessboard made for mountains. She was vaguely aware it was below freezing outside. She could have sat at the edge of the bed and stared all night, with the clown paintings on the walls looking over her shoulder. It was not the gaudy atmosphere outside the door she minded. If she were not here for work, she might have enjoyed herself, but when was anything not "work"?

Then she went out, into that hypnotic sea of machines and spinning sevens. Old-timers sat there with entire rows to themselves, playing two or more quarter slots at once. When she used to spend her days and nights in these kinds of places, she was always on the job and never considered herself a gambler. When she did give it a whirl, knowing full well the game within the game, sometimes she had the touch, sometimes not. She had done the probability study, and she acknowledged some people had a good time with it, but she was not one of them. Whatever it was she came here for, really just to be in the mountains, breathing in the altitude, no more than that, it was not so she could throw her money away. She was not like Lincoln. It was not that she found it immoral; it was that she had done the calculations and decided against it.

Well, she was here now and for once had some time to kill.

She took the elevator to the mezzanine and looked at some crystals. Did people really come here to buy that stuff? Maybe if you were drunk or had just won thirty dollars. She thought of a show, but was tired from the drive, and thought she would just turn in after dinner, then find something to do in the morning, when most everyone would still be sleeping. She crossed the length of the indoor mall to the replica mining site, where giant rig wheels turned in a continuous dusk under the dome. The crowds were only growing thicker as it got closer to mealtime.

Piping out of the fake sky was an old Cantonese song. Back when she was in Taiwan, she could not have imagined this happening here, but now like the rest of her life, it was. There were no other signs of the Lunar New Year. There was so little in this part of the world to remind you. Tomorrow would not be the wrong Lunar New Year they celebrated a week later in the casinos, when Cantopop singers sang live and all the buffets served what was supposed to be Chinese food. The one clue, which she should have noticed, that it was in fact the actual Lunar New Year was that there were not a lot of Chinese people around. This was abnormal. On a regular weekend like this you would be elbowing through them, or more likely, getting elbowed. The Chinese loved to gamble, everyone knew that, but the real Lunar New Year was the one time of year they went someplace else. Nobody knew this.

She considered taking in the circus acts while watching the procession of men in cowboy hats and big metal buckles, sunburned teenagers in ski jackets, and families in matching sweat clothes.

Looking over the dining options from the menus posted outside each buffet, she wondered how it was everything seemed unappetizing. It was probably no accident. Here in this country there was some method behind everything. They liked to consider everything down to the last detail, their so-called "data," when at the same time, you would be shocked, once everything had been taken into account, how slipshod the execution could be. They could plan for every last stray bit of probability in order to reach the irrefutable, then would just half-ass their way through the actual work. She had seen it happen enough times to expect it, and in some sense, she understood.

Over a meal that consisted of a little bit of everything, she flipped through one of the free entertainment guides that were stacked everywhere. She considered Carson City. It was listed under "day trips," places it had never occurred to her to go. It was true, whenever she came to this town she would never get past the main drag. But now: Galena Creek, Washoe, Genoa, Pyramid Lake. That latter could have been Tibet, a turquoise lake in the high, snowy desert, with coelacanth inside its waters. How was that possible? It was something out of science fiction.

She flipped the page to Virginia City, perusing the photographs of carny billboards on a winding mountain road, beckoning her to tourist traps with names like Bucket of Blood. She

was surprised that kind of come-on still existed and was in-
trigued. According to the article, the once-glittering Paris of the
West had preserved its original layout clinging to the edge of
a rock cliff, and in her mind's eye she pictured San Francisco's
Chinatown, which likewise hung off the side of a steep slope.
In fact, the article went on, Virginia City once boasted one of
the largest Chinese communities in America. She imagined at-
tractions, or maybe just a plaque, commemorating the existence
of these people, with their ducks hanging in windows, cluttered
general-goods stores, Taoist shrines, and cabins filled with the
clatter of opera and mahjong, but there would in all likelihood
be no sign of them anymore. If she went, she might well be the
only Chinese person in town.[11]

Entire libraries had been published on the subject, to explain
what could not be explained, but none of those books managed
to get down what her stories of the Cultural Revolution did.
Despite her precedence, her model was somehow not followed,
or in what attempts there were, the focus was misdirected. It
was not the slightly maudlin plots that produced their power,
but the observations of a new, revolutionary reality. It was as if
each line were being tested for its veracity, the purpose of the
writing to confirm what had been experienced and in that way
lock it away forever. The sentences, and thus the fictions they
accumulated into, felt as if they were snapping shut; it was the
way she was to go about her business deals in later life.

If in her new book the subject evaded her earlier methods,
it was because she did not have history to serve as ballast; she

---

[11] From *The Lost Lives of Lena Wu.*

had to convince the reader of her own gravity as a storyteller of far lighter events. Not that a man's life was ever a light matter, but there was no agreement around the relevance of the subject; the pointlessness of émigré life had been a shared complaint by what few critics there were of her recent work. As a result, her approach fluttered as she tried to recalibrate. There were points where those fine observations simply began to stack one upon the other. If her attention or energy flagged, they decayed into their original fragmented state, as if one were only reading the preparatory notes. Perhaps it would not have been so bad if she had simply transcribed those jottings, since I was more curious about them anyway, but the book also shifted into workaday novelistic modes: dropped-in transitions, things shown instead of told, characters' dialogue or inner thoughts making explicit what had already been picked up by the ear and sense. The sentences continued their forward march, sometimes knocked off course by the author's arbitrary time shifts, with only the vague sense, or hope, a structure might emerge. Then again, what else did a reader read for?

In the telling, Lena was a stand-in for struggle itself. There was something wrong about this conceit, though. She might be defined by the struggle, but the reverse was not true: the struggle was not Lena. Yvonne was challenging one of the fundamental dilemmas faced by the novelist, that the characters that made the story "work" were not the characters one should like to see written about. Rather than craft people that only served the mechanics of the plot, she provided something else, which was all fine and good, except that Lena was miscast.

I was not reading for the aesthetic experience, anyway. I was trying to determine how much of the book was based on the truth. The parts I could corroborate held up under this test, but I could not say, based on this, if the rest should get a pass. Those passages unfamiliar to me may have just been contrived to tie things up. There may have been clues in the mosquitoes, lawns, and trees, in the buses picking up passengers not in San Francisco's Chinatown but in the drab southeast corner of the city. The drop-off point in the parking lot of a huge ethnic mall, in front of a popular banh mi chain, was too idiosyncratic a detail not to have been based on somebody's reality. On the other hand, I found the closing chapters short on illuminating detail and mystified by psychology.

It was a love story, after all: in the end, she got what she wanted and lost the men in her life. It was an easy equation, one that did not seem to have come from the author's sense of purpose, but an editorial intervention to bring the narrative and characters to a close.

I looked up from my reading to the empty bowls scattered in front of me. Behind me hovered a queue of ghost-faces belonging to the hungry customers aiming to take my seat at the bar.

She was sharing, with two students, a detached one-story house with a brown lawn, the kind of structure that America had instead of ruins. It was a slow river city, with flat streets and a confusion of interchanges. Coming from LA, she appreciated the trees, including the one right outside her window. She stared out at it through the wire screen when she needed to clear her head, slapping mosquitoes and listening to the sound of traffic in the heat.

Unlike LA, it was an unromantic city, which nevertheless remained a mystery to her—she never quite figured out how to dress like a local and always assumed she looked like someone from out of town, if not from out of the country—but that must have helped her streamline her thinking. The idea that worked was something anyone could have come up with. This was the beauty of business, a principle she learned from watching Rafael, who applied his intelligence to everything he did. For a long time she failed in everything as he did, emulating him, finding herself drawn to the same methods, over and over, as the mind made adjustments in order not to make the same mistakes, which only served to fool itself into thinking there would be a better outcome this time. Now she knew better. Try a different way, but *stupider*, more cowardly. Just take your customers where they wanted to go.

She secured the financing. At this point, fear was no longer part of the calculus of risk and reward. When had she lost it? She always assumed it was because of what happened to Rafael, but now realized it had been a more recent development. What she mistook for courage at the time had only been shock; moreover, it was the same shock everyone else experienced. What those who believed she had been the one to push him into the bullet's path did not know was that she had not been there. She only found out about what had happened to Rafael from the police. She could not remember his last words to her. Everything from there was blank.

Once the route was announced, by word of mouth and some well-placed flyers, customers filled the buses by themselves, because it was a no-brainer to get these city dwellers to where they wanted to go, some of whom never needed to drive, or were too old to, or otherwise never left their one or two neighborhood haunts. The rise of the tribal casinos convinced her competitors that there was no reason to take passengers as far as Reno. In the winter especially, the "hump" was the costliest part of the trip, so it became the most underserved as soon as everyone did the risk math. Her simplistic business strategy, and courage, then, was to go where they were not.

Eventually she abandoned the first half of the route, did pickups on tribal land, then consolidated. It was too early to say if she was right. It always was, though wasn't it? By not picking up passengers in the city, she cut fixed costs and focused her time between Auburn and Reno. She moved around, on either side of the state border, building her network.

There were places to go. You would be surprised what got people interested once it was shown to them in the right way. She found an older gentleman who ran walking tours out of a Taoist temple in the heritage part of town, what they called the "Joss House." He referred riders to her. She understood now that her customers were the slightly more adventurous ones, the ones who wanted to find out what was on the other side of the hill. Did they know about the Chinatown in Virginia City? Surprisingly, some of the younger overseas tourists were curious about it. Before long her number was on a handwritten sign taped to his front door.

She rode with them sometimes, a round trip a day with the occasional overnighter, to make sure things were running all right and to get a sense of the customer experience. It went fine until Christmas. Those vehicles were not meant to be hauled, like pioneer wagons, which didn't fare so well either, over Donner Pass in a snap winter storm.

There was the slow settling knot of concern, somewhere in the exact center of the trunk of her body, a vestige of that primordial fear of the elements, that one might, for example, freeze.

Before it became a mundane inconvenience, once the authorities showed up, as they would, on the shoulder of a major highway, she caught a hint of that descent.

On the one hand, it was too late to do anything about it. On the other was the twitch to do something, anything, under the scent of the pine trees. There might be minor injuries. If she was not hurt and someone else was, what would she say? What was her liability? She did not have this spiral of panic when Rafael was killed. She did not see herself as responsible then, even though she was to find out everybody else did and she was to deal with the consequences before she even knew what caused them.

This, on the other hand, was an everyday occurrence. It was just that it normally happened with cars, not buses. Passengers trickled out, dazed, one bloody nose among them, screaming red at her as she gazed across the Sierra backcountry. The vehicle would need to be repaired, but it was not totaled.

She could do nothing but wait for help to arrive. She stared into the sky over the horizon of the road. Snow was falling out of it. The rhythm of the mounting flurries was a kind of language. It was in the pace of this falling, in the moments between scatterings, that she found a relief from fear.

It was exhausting. Fighting through missteps everyday was no longer stultifying, nor did she try to escape them anymore. All she could do was meet them head-on. The tension in her chest would always be there. It had become a way of life, not that that helped her sleep better. Something else made it bearable as it diffused into black space, the descent into that unimagined opening.[12]

---

[12] Ibid.

{11}

THE CITY WAS A DREAM, up and down these hills, in particular
the middle of the day, in the middle of the week. Often when
the sun was veiled, one lost sense of what time of day it was,
what day it was. Yvonne knew the story of every house she
passed, commenting from behind the wheel that one of them
got a new paint job over the summer, another was fixing a window, and another needed the services of a professional arborist.
She did the impossible, finding a curbside parking spot by her
office, its storefront windows flush to the sidewalk and stick-
ered with the latest neighborhood for-sales and sale-pendings.
The picture windows let light in, and on the sill sat several pots
of succulents. Her messy desk exhibited a working fax machine
and a gray cat where the sunlight caught its corner. The neigh-
bor's, she explained, as she dropped it outside and propped the
front door open, so it could let in the breeze from the street
which ran straight to the bay.

As I sat down on the other side of the desk from her, looking through the open door to a faint band of blue, I disclosed
the purpose of my calling, but only got halfway through the

explanation before she confirmed, yes, that apartment had been in the novel, not as a setting for any scene, but a lever in the narrative. I nodded, remembering. She had never been inside it, she confessed, nor even driven by, but learned how Rafael ended up buying it, as part of her research. This had all been after our trip; if she had known then, she would have wanted us to visit there first thing. What was funny was that, once she corroborated the facts, she could not be bothered to go, because it had not occurred to her that Lena would dare to continue living there.

About Lena: she had sat right where I was sitting now. It had not been revelatory when she visited, and anyway it had been after Yvonne sent in her manuscript. How it happened was by means of a net laid by the novelist months ago, when Yvonne put word out through her industry contacts to send the femme fatale her way. None the wiser, Lena arrived thinking she was only there for answers about tenant rights and lawyer referrals, which, now that Yvonne thought about it, should have been the tip-off she was still leasing the place and moreover was having trouble with her landlord. Of course Yvonne did not let on she had just written a book about her, which would have been the most awkward possible confession to make under the circumstances. Probably, she guessed, I was curious as to her appearance: a classical beauty, a Lin Daiyu type, if I understood the reference, although Yvonne found her face rather exotic for a Chinese. On first look she would have been mistaken for an FOB by the way she dressed, not someone who had been in the States more than ten years. Maybe that was a byproduct of living in Southern California? She was not as young as the media had made her out to be; Rafael had not been dating twenty-year-olds. Yvonne took her to be in her late thirties. One last, curious thing was that she clearly did not like Yvonne. Since the two of them were barely acquainted, it may have simply been intuitive disdain, the protagonist sensing the designs of her author, or, less fancifully, something to do with Yvonne's profession. For her part, since she knew so much about her subject already, she could not have an unbiased opinion.

To see her: that was what we had taken the trip for, wasn't it? Well, now she had, but it produced in her something like the opposite effect than she hoped. She found out she already knew what she needed for her book and that this woman was exactly what my father imagined her to be. Seeing and hearing her did jog some memories, but they were just of the media coverage from that unwelcome time. Shortly after the meeting, she got sucked back into her work, her real work; the novel and Lena receded from her priorities. Really she had not thought about them much until I showed up today.

I found it off-putting that an artist such as herself could file away her creation just like that, the quarry we had been after for so long, but I did not say anything. Instead, I took this as my opportunity to discuss the compositional process of her novel, which after all was the real reason for my visit. If she had not spoken to Lena until after she had written the book, how did she fill in the gaps of what we knew of Lena's life?

It was true, she replied, she had been on the verge of giving up writing that book and would have, if two things had not happened. One of them was that she followed up with

Lincoln, who then mailed her a packet of Lena's letters. None of them were very long, as Lena had a discreet and rather elliptical writing style; nonetheless, she let slip enough life-detail that Yvonne could puzzle the pieces together. Chronologically, they covered the time from when she and Lincoln separated to when she settled in Northern California, which was a godsend, because that was exactly the period when Lena's life went dark and Yvonne had nothing else to go on.

I confessed I found these to be the best parts of the book, and no wonder; they were based on the closest thing we had to Lena's own testimony. When I asked if I could see those letters, she responded evasively, saying that they were at home, not in her office, but that she would show me someday.[13]

The other piece came by serendipity. With those letters, she now had a framework for the aftermath of the central incident in her novel, but she still lacked definition of the buildup to it. This was where talking to the widow would have helped, but Margaret was steadfast in refusing to meet her or to grant an interview with her son. All else she could find on that period of Lena's life fell under the category of rumors, and Yvonne was ready to add her own contribution to that mountain of lies

---

[13] During the preparation of this translation, I actually contacted Yvonne Fung about those letters, but despite making promises similar to the one she makes as a character in my father's manuscript, she never came forward. At this point, I suspect Yvonne never had them and the versions in her book's appendix are free re-creations of what we read in Ventura. Her motive to claim access to them, however many of them there may be, is apparent; they are the provenance of her book's veracity, a trait more important to a text with pretensions to fiction than any other kind.

when she ran into a friend of hers, a fellow realtor, at a home showing. Shop talk was her actual job; unlike her other occupation, this one did not oblige her to sit at a desk, but to be out and about. They got to chatting, and while it turned out she had nothing to provide by way of business, her friend did let her know that one of her former clients had been Rafael. What she then disclosed, in the ensuing hours after they closed up the showing and went for coffee, meandered beyond the usual gossip; she mapped out an entire dynamic, glimpsed from the privileged vantage point of a commissioned broker who must play silent and private witness to a couple's agonizing decisions over large sums of money.

Before going on, she paused and, as if reminded by her own mention of Margaret, asked if the widow was on the Society's mailing list. It was too late now, but it had just occurred to her that her newsletter article might have caused offense. As a donor she did receive them, I explained, in fact I had stamped the envelope myself, but I highly doubted she read it or even gave the sheet a quick glance. Yvonne then asked if it was true I was working for her. Wondering how such news spread, I simply replied, no, not unless you counted running errands on my father's behalf to be employment. She was still concerned that someone would bring the article to Margaret's attention, but I reassured her that if there had been any controversy I would have heard about it by now. She did want to thank me for running the piece. It had been an important exercise for her, maybe even more than the novel itself, and she had to fight her editor to include the introduction, even though the scandal had been the reason the publisher agreed to bring the book out in the first place. Once the sensation around the case died down, they felt referring to it would make its contents seem stale. None of this mattered to her. It had been perhaps the most difficult of her books to write, and in the end she realized what it lacked was a straight account of the facts. The newspapers never responsibly reported them, and her novel hid them behind the guise of fiction. I had given her an opportunity to get out the truth. How many writers have that chance? Very few.

Her discourse sounded grandiose for a couple of columns of airy reading, as I remembered it, but I welcomed her gratitude.

When I asked if Lena might be open to answering some questions, she laughed. What did I want to ask? Would I try to get her to say Rafael was a good man after all and that she was wrong to mistreat him? Or was I going on my father and Margaret's behalf to ask for Rafael's money back? Of course she could put me in touch, for whatever I wanted.

As for representing the sale of the apartment, which she already knew was what I had come to ask, she would do it. She wanted to help, of course, but her primary motive, she confessed, was that she wanted to speak to the tenant again. You mean kick her out, don't you? I asked. Well, that too, but she had a feeling Lena would be open to negotiation. For one thing, she did not fall under the category of "tenant," with all the attendant rights. That would give us leverage, and Lena would be even more willing if my father were to throw some money her way.

Rafael was not the first one she talked to. It was the other, Lena, who called, saying they had met at a party and then contradicting herself later by saying she had gotten her number through a referral. That was not a good first impression, but the woman's bad lies seemed so deliberate they came across as shrewd—or an attempt to give the appearance of shrewdness, which was as notable.

When they all finally met in person, both members of the couple were present. He was thin, with thick gray hair, in a tweed jacket and yellow sweater vest. The first thing Lena did was break out a blue realtor's map, marked with different highlighters in some kind of color code for the neighborhoods they were interested in. Based on the range they were willing to pay, their goals were not realistic. The market was not as hot as it was a few years ago, but it had not cooled off much. Rafael just grinned that grin of his and said they would like to take a look anyway, implying if they found something they liked he would make up the difference.

Later she got the hint they were lovers, although they insisted they were looking for something for business. Lena did not seem to be an employee, and she was the one taking the lead on the search, as if it were going to be *her* house. As they were herded through the routine, touring open homes, getting to know neighborhoods they had not heard of, sometimes being picked up and driven to the spot, sometimes being met there, the usual tensions in couples, at first simmering below the surface, came out under pressure, deeper emotions than what one would expect from businesspeople only interested in a corporate apartment. Everything in the history of one's life comes out when picking one's own house, and Lena was all over the place. Rafael for the most part was deferential, but it seemed he had something in mind.

Lena really wanted a single-family house, not an apartment. Her priorities were space and recency. If that was the case, she suggested, they should be looking in the suburbs, or if they wanted something closer to culture and nightlife, lofts and condos. They did not seem to understand reality, something she ran up against a lot. After all, San Francisco did not fit newcomers' notions of California. Those Victorians gave off an air of luxury from the outside, but inside they were eccentric, a quintessential local trait. This was not Brentwood. It was, by West Coast standards, an old city. Coming from Asia, they found anything more than ten years old repulsively out of date. Such would-be buyers did not understand the city was not designed to be updated, since earthquakes and economic crashes did that work already, so she often ended up steering people to the Peninsula, or at least the avenues, where there were more schools, flat yards, and postwar housing stock. Many of them just gave up in the end. It sounded as if Lena had her heart set on some place near the downtown core, in the trendier spots, which was to say, not its Chinese ones.

While they drove around, Lena in front, Rafael in back, Lena complained nonstop about how exhausting she found the whole process. She was critical of the houses, did not think any of them were worth it. Not a good listener, she tuned out any explanations of market value and buyer behavior. "Just show me the houses." Rafael was not like that. He was fascinated, maybe more amused, by it all. He asked questions that sounded innocent enough, but there was an agenda behind them. What that was, was hard to tell.

Slowly he took her into his confidence. He set up calls and a few meetings, without Lena around. The tone of these conversations was different. He wanted to get straight information, mostly financial. There was an understanding she was to keep it discreet, Lena's existence above all, since they moved in the same circles, but it was a small world, and she got the sense people already knew about the paramour, but maybe not, as she did, firsthand. Amid the swirling rumors, he was surprisingly good at keeping things compartmentalized.

Once she called him to see if they would be interested in checking out a new listing. There would be a Tuesday realtors' showing before the weekend open, and they were probably taking bids right after that. Rafael was noticeably irritated and told her maybe it was not the right time after all and they should take a break. This gentle brush-off came out of the blue. Maybe something had happened between him and Lena. She did not know, but it was not her business. It was normal, especially for first-time lookers, to hit a wall, and she knew how to steer them through. She suggested she check back, maybe after the new year. He said all right.

A few days later, though, he called back. He had seen a listing. He was interested in taking a look. Would she come with him? She immediately checked the realtor database and told him it was a condo. Yes, he knew that, but between him and her, he thought this would be better. Don't worry, he would work on Lena.

When they met her there, Lena fell in love with the place. She reminded them a single-family home would make a better investment. Rafael just nodded and did not ask about the HOA fees. Lena was brash and stubborn, but for the bigger decisions, she went along with him. His company took out the loan, and the transfer of the down payment came from the company bank account.[14]

---

[14] From *The Lost Lives of Lena Wu.*

There was one last thing I wanted to ask her. She said Lena was exactly as my father imagined her to be. What did she mean by that? I believed, I told her, she was referring to the final scene of her novel, which mirrored a passage near the end of my father's memoir about my sister. In it, the latter brought my sister into an aging, beat-up Chinese restaurant in Nevada; a subtly mysterious encounter would occur there. Actually I was present too, if hardly mentioned, while as a reader the scene had always stayed with me, since it was not at all clear why my father had seen fit to include it. In addition, I vaguely recalled a similar trip we actually took, which would suggest the scene was fictional, because the person we met in it never appeared in real life. It struck me now that the woman in the restaurant shared characteristics with Lena Wu, such as working as a flight attendant and card dealer. It seemed Yvonne had picked up on this odd echo through the decades, by alluding to it at the end of *her* book, where she had her main character visit what seemed to be that same restaurant. It could not be a coincidence. For most readers, it would be, as in my father's book, a cryptic scene and probably an unsatisfying end to the story, but I thought I knew the key. What did she think was going on here? It was not as if anybody had read my father's memoir, or if they did, recalled that particular moment, so as an allusion it would be recognized only among the happy few. Instead what she seemed to be doing was invoking the strange pre-appearance of Lena Wu in a text that anticipated the real person by thirty years.

She replied she was not really following me and confessed she had never finished my father's book. She had read the first few chapters, like everybody else, in order to comment on it when asked to at the time of its publication, but never got to the part I was talking about. This was the way it was when writers had to see each other and talk about each other's work, one of the burdens of literary life, and she hoped I would not hold it against her. Although now that I had mentioned it, she was curious to go back and read that section.

I had not anticipated this answer. I had been certain she had written an homage to my father's book. What were the odds that both of them would end with the same setting, with the mysterious walk-on in one reappearing by chance as the protagonist in the other—a character based on real life, no less?

At this moment, her phone rang, and the cat made its way back inside. Yvonne abruptly snapped back into deal-making mode, where perhaps she was happiest of all, and in this way maybe did understand the subject of her novel. After I went out, having told her I could catch the bus, I could not help feeling that I would never see those letters she promised nor find out if she picked up my father's book again, if she ever did in the first place.

I sorted through the probabilities. The most likely, of course, was that Yvonne was lying, or more charitably put, misremembering. She had read the scene, forgotten about it, then sifted it from her subconscious, rewriting it in that delusive trance we call storytelling, convinced she was being original. As for the incarnation of Lena in my father's book, I would have to revisit the passage to confirm, but it was probably coincidental, colored by my recent reading of Yvonne's portrait.

But that would seem too easy an out, and for some reason did not sit well with me as I made my way home. There were two other possibilities of a more fantastic kind. The first one, perhaps all together conceivable and that had been slowly dawning on me even as I went through Yvonne's book, was that Lena Wu, as my father and Yvonne understood her, did not exist. She was a phantom of, first, my father's obsession with Rafael's justice, and second, Yvonne's obsession with her own past. Of course a person of that name existed, it was just that none of us had gotten to know her. The Lena of collective imagination was embellished by the gossip surrounding Rafael's death, revived by my father in disgusted reaction to that gossip, and brought to fruition by Yvonne's writerly professionalism. I saw now how she did not even need to know about my father's book to get as far as she did, for the conception had been in the air all around us, and it would only take the spark of conscious effort to write a book (twice!) to bring the creature to life.

The second was more monstrous, but was what I found myself toying with in the days that followed. Somehow through their independent stumbling efforts, Yvonne and my father had found their way into the stream of literature, that is, of literary time, wherein texts on opposite ends of eternity speak to one another and literature, even our very minor case of it, was for all time, having already been written, and it was only a matter for our writers, working in the dark, to bring some piece of them to the light. If they were sincere in their efforts, then what they brought back was not art but a fragment of reality. And what reality did they dig up? An immigrant father's regret. For when he encountered "Lena" in that restaurant, he saw his daughter

as he wished her to be and not, despite the hundred or so preceding pages about a father's love, someone who was funda-
mentally a cipher to him. He constructed a replacement, since
he was, after all, a writer, one whom he thought he knew better
and one, years down the road, whom he would lose control of
too, as we already knew.

{12}

{133}

We arrived at the former offices of the *Territorial Enterprise*. It was closed, but there was a plaque out front.

MARK TWAIN, WHO GREATLY ENRICHED THE LITERATURE OF THE WEST, STARTED HIS CAREER AS A WRITER IN THIS BUILDING IN 1862 ON THE EDITORIAL STAFF OF THE TERRITORIAL ENTERPRISE.

I had always thought of Twain as a Southerner, but this in no way qualified as the South. If anything, it was the classic setting for a "Western," and I now realized Twain must have been a Westerner too and somehow made it out to this rock desert; it must not have been easy to get around the country in those days. I did not know at the time that he had lived in San Francisco too, where, alas, there is no commemorative plaque. In my mind, Jack London was the most famous writer associated with the Bay Area. In Oakland there is still a replica of London's shack, just as in Chengdu you can find a copy of Tu Fu's thatched hut. The message of both is the same: *Good writing comes from bad fate*. Tu Fu wrote that.

So Twain had worked at a newspaper, this very one before us. I could not imagine a place that could be less conducive to writing. As you stared into the Great Basin, all you would want to do was set out and if not prospect for silver then simply walk as far as your legs could take you. I too had wanted to be a journalist in my youth. It seemed the most agreeable compromise between an idle life of letters and a practical way to make a living, but my father talked me out of it. That is a mild way of putting it. I majored in civil engineering.

I brought the children into a bookstore. This would be our last stop in town.

The main display at the front of the store showed off books of regional interest, including a collection of self-published pamphlets by local amateur historians, such as one on "The Chinese of Comstock." But I was more drawn to the back of the room, which served as a kind of museum, with an antique gold balance scale on display, delivered, read the placard, from London to San Francisco, then brought back east over the Sierras—to join on that shelf, a hundred and forty years later, what was claimed to be the first light bulbs and phonograph in the city. What interested me most, though, as an engineer, were the sectional cutaway maps of Sutro Tunnel, the six-mile-long drainage tunnel running through the mines termiting below the streets of the city. Sitting next to it was a life-size dummy of Mark Twain dressed in that white suit and string tie, legs crossed, looking a bit put out by the player piano squeezing him into a corner.

This second encounter with the writer finally reminded me of an incident from my college days, in retrospect both funny but also more terrifying than when I experienced it. You, who are reading this in traditional Chinese characters, know the backdrop to this scene as well as I, the incomprehensibly frightening news coming out of the mainland at the time in which, according to the official government line, five thousand years of civilization were being ground to dust. We were the last bulwark against barbarity, the defenders of Confucian principles.

The men who came to my dormitory room had been tipped off by someone—I always suspected my roommate—who had misread the author attribution of my translation of *Huckleberry Finn*. Due to a lack of cultural literacy, he had taken the Chinese characters that were the transliteration of "Mark" to mean "Marx."[15]

Once I cleared that up, the men, already uneasy in our cloistered campus atmosphere, were abashed and politely apologized to the person who back then was still the young scholar. Who knew what they would have done if the situation were just a bit different?

I cannot remember ever getting through *Huckleberry Finn* in Chinese. That incident is the only reason I remember ever owning a copy of it. If I had read it at all, the words must have passed straight through me. Years later, I did read *Tom Sawyer*, in English, and then *Huckleberry Finn* in the original, but the rendition of dialect was too much, and I gave up without getting very far. From then on I never believed those former classmates of mine who claimed to have read it all the way through in the original, never mind something like Faulkner. On top of that, they were all too happy to jump in at a moment's notice to carry forth on the importance of *Huckleberry Finn*, or Faulkner, whether to themselves or to world literature, speaking on its behalf, when it occurred to me you cannot really get what was going on in those books

---

[15] "Mark" as in "Mark Twain" is typically transliterated into the Chinese characters *mǎ kè* (the same *mǎ*, incidentally, that is the character for "horse") which forms the first two characters of *mǎ kè sī*—the transliteration of "Marx."

unless you were a real American, as my children are. (But neither Americans nor my children read books.) All other opinions I am suspicious of. It does not matter, because these conversations are never so much about the contents of the books as what they stand for, the greatness and democracy of American literature, like the land itself. Yes, great and democratic, but I suspect those works to be more esoteric, and exclusive, than anything to be found in the classical Chinese canon.

The kids were preoccupied sorting through piles of rocks the store sold as souvenirs, but I had a sudden urge to leave. I did not know what drew me out, but once on the street the cold was invigorating. The town, which had streams of tourists coursing through it before we went inside, was now barren, as if they had all been chased off by the arrival of some imminent threat, man or beast or just the slashing mountain winds and impending darkness.

The girl said she was hungry, so we looked for a place to eat that was not a saloon. After waddling a couple of blocks in our ski jackets, we turned a corner, went down the hill, and came upon a Chinese restaurant. It seemed to be the only one in town. It did not look like the kind of place you would really want to eat in, more like a tourist trap. The plaque by its entrance claimed the alley heading sharply downhill led into what had once been the city's flourishing Chinatown. It did not look like the dirt lot at the end of the alley could fit one-third of the city's population, as the plaque claimed.

I took a few steps closer to the restaurant window. It was hard to see through the words CHINESE RESTAURANT painted on glass in chop-suey font and the reflective glare of the snow on the street, but I could see a person, a woman, not a dummy, wearing a red cheongsam, the sole remnant of this historic neighborhood. Maybe it was a costume for tourists for the new year? She stood behind a wooden bar in an aquarium-world of vinyl booths and green walls. No one else was there. She could have been the proprietress. To stay in business, I thought, she would have had to be resourceful. I did not want to go in, but the girl, who cut such a sapient figure on stage, but was otherwise just a kid, kept whining.

While the two kids slurped down wontons, the proprietress got to talking. At first we were caught up in that awkward dilemma familiar to all of us who find ourselves living overseas for a certain length of time and confronting another Chinese face: should we be speaking in some language other than English? And who will bring this up first? I was wary of using Mandarin, thinking the greater likelihood she was Cantonese, so I was surprised, and relieved, to find out she was from, of all places, Taiwan. In fact, we knew people in common. Her path here—by which I meant to this broken-down restaurant in the middle of nowhere, where our paths somehow crossed—was different from mine. She had worked as a stewardess, then a card dealer in the casinos. From there she managed to save enough money to buy this establishment, which had been on the verge of closing.

"But it's no good. I'm going to sell it. You interested? The location's awful, off the main drag, and the down season's too long. When I am open, I'm tied up all day. It'd be different if I had help, but it doesn't make enough money for that."

"When you mentioned you were the owner, my first thought was you had some help."

"No, it's not like that. I'm a self-made woman. Or trying to be."

"I admire you. I suppose it's more and more the case, in this country, anyway, and my daughter will one day be like you, a self-reliant American. But I think we all need to rely on one another, ultimately."

"I learned the hard way it's better just to do things yourself. Besides, it's not so bad staring out at these rocks all day. Just kidding! I'll be moving on soon."

"Well *I* like it out here. Nice to come out to the open country once in a while."

"The mountains follow you around here. And because there aren't other people to dump your feelings on, you end up talking to them."

Behind her was an oddity for a Chinese restaurant: a bookshelf. I squinted at the spines. All the titles were in English, and I didn't recognize a single one. They all seemed to be about cowboys. Despite the friendly, familiar chatter, for it was always welcome to hear that accent far from home, no matter how long one had been away, I began to think of a way out. It was not that I was growing tired of her, but I sensed something weird coming out from within that peculiar nineteenth-century structure. I heard sounds from where was supposed to be a kitchen, despite what she said about being alone, alternating between hushed conversation and the unmistakable click of mahjong tiles. Momentarily I thought of those stories in *Liaozhai*, where the wontons the kids were eating turn out to be a soup of human heads and this was not a restaurant but an abandoned temple. And she . . . ?

"You don't see a lot of single dads around here."

"My wife's back at the casino. She likes gambling. I don't."

"Well, it's nice you got your children out of there to do some sightseeing."

"You said that was once your line of work, right?"

"I didn't like it. I used to gamble. I don't anymore."

"Because it's rigged?"

"I wouldn't say that. More like, 'House always wins.'"

"I don't understand why people get enjoyment out of leaving things to chance."

"You and I are the same way. But it's not chance. Your children are very well-behaved, by the way. They seem very bright. The boy has intelligent eyes."

"His sister's the talented one, actually. Some people say she's a prodigy."

"Is that so? Are you?"

My daughter shrugged and mimed playing a violin to explain. And then, as if to provide a better answer, she began whining again, this time about leaving. She did not want to miss the evening circus show.

"I'm writing a book about her. When it's published, I'll bring it over, so you can leave it on that shelf, as a memento of our visit."

She looked back as if seeing the shelf for the first time. "Please do that."

I left my number. She seemed isolated out here, I said, but now whenever she was in the Bay Area, she could look us up if she was in the mood for company or just a taste of home. Never mind what I said about self-reliance: we immigrants stick together. I did not expect her to contact me, though, and she never did.[16]

After coming out of the red desert and over Geiger Summit, there seemed to be only one street in town. Unable at first to pin down the distinctly odd impression the city made, after cruising past a few blocks of weathered two- and three-story façades, she

---

16 From *My Daughter the Prodigy* (Wǒ de tiāncái nǚ'ér).

attributed it to a matter of proportion. It had not been redone for cars. Surrounded by effectively nothing, particularly to the east, which stretched, for all purposes, to eternity, the brick and clapboard structures and hilly streets meant for humans and horses were nonetheless packed tightly. Its lines were neither clean nor geometric. Still, it gave the impression of being *built*. It was not an "old town" restoration. She imagined remote villages in China as something like this, different construction materials, but the same handmade feel.

After passing by the *Territorial Enterprise*, she walked a few more blocks down the main drag. In a way that reminded her of San Francisco's Chinatown, the town was built on a rugged slope, its north-south streets forming tiers to the sky, and instead of following "C" Street to its end, or rather to where it just diffused into the landscape, she took a turn that felt like falling off a cliff. A sign indicated a dirt lot another block downhill to be formerly this city's Chinatown, although it seemed impossible it could have harbored the number of inhabitants claimed on the sign.

Then she stood in front of a plate glass window with the letters CHINESE RESTAURANT hand-painted on it. Through the glass were green vinyl booths, green-painted walls, and a vintage wooden bar, with a bookshelf and shrine on the other side of it. There was nobody inside, but smoke curled out of the Kwan Kung shrine, indicating a recent presence.

A passage just wide enough for one person bordered one side of the building. It opened onto the delivery alley behind the commercial street, where the businesses could not be told from one another. All the doors were closed and nobody was around. But somebody, or something, had been there not long ago. At her feet, in the snow, were shreds of red paper.

The scraps of spent firecrackers on ice melting in the warming morning air were a paltry pile compared to those no doubt by now filling squares and alleys in San Francisco and Taipei. Whoever set them off had already disappeared into the background, perhaps gone into the vast underground labyrinth below the city.

She found herself climbing uphill. Ahead was an open space. It faced east from the edge of town, revealing the reality behind that backlot set of a street: canyons, cliffs, spires, and shapes, uninhabited in all directions. It could have been the Grand Canyon, with outlaws and Indians hiding in its folds, awaiting their last stand. She knew it did not really go on forever like that. At some point it must have flattened and grown monotonous with scattered buildings entering the picture, but from this vantage point it seemed infinite.

Space diffuses what haunts us in time. Time builds up and becomes simultaneous and makes things chaotic, but distance creates order. It occurred to her to keep going. It was a perfectly normal thing to do. Rafael had tried it too, which he would not have regretted if he had been given the chance.

But she decided to turn around. It was too much to think about, all of it, the rest of the world, and best go back to what she knew better.[17]

---

[17] From *The Lost Lives of Lena Wu.*

{13}

It did not pass unnoticed that Mike would not enter his old boss's office alone and waited for all of us to go in before he did. As much as he had once swallowed his tongue in Rafael's presence, this probably had less to do with any persistent obligation of deference on his part than it was simply being superstitious, a trait of those who lived by numbers; my father had once mentioned that people at the lab were like that. My father, however, was not one of them and had no such compunctions as he took his old friend's chair behind the desk, as I had before, and chose to hold the small meeting there, instead of in one of the larger rooms. The gathering consisted of him, Mike, Eileen, and myself.

They spoke with the resolve that came with power when it was actually possessed and exercised, and the logistical discussion was enacted with the economy of the one mind they had become; for once, Mike did not have much to add. They dug out numbers, made snap calls to excise this or that fixed cost, and communicated in telegraphic phrases or code, snippets that slid off their tongues. Even if I was not always sure what they were referring to, it was obvious collectively they knew their way around the recesses of the business by now. There was a gallows humor in the back of those phrases, too, necessary for the lethal work. After all, these were people's livelihoods they were scratching off with a quip, salaries for those who had made sacrifices, in some cases for a decade or two, with the understanding of an unspoken mutual pact. Sometimes Mike would murmur indecipherably in a sarcastic tone, in response to nobody.

As the new budget came together, roughly, it became apparent to me that, for all his so-called reliability, my father had little experience running a business. He did not know how fragile any sense of stability was and how, when things collapsed, they collapsed all at once. Besides the hidden expenditures unearthed by Eileen, Mike went on to describe investments he had scattered throughout the financial statements with his usual sleight of hand. This was possible when revenue growth was steep enough to sugarcoat everything, but now, with the departure of the company's biggest client, revenue was drying up, and they had no choice but to amortize those losses, for Rafael never picked winners. This day was something the old man must have seen coming, but could never admit to himself, much less to others. If such calamities occurred in sequence, he could mask them, but together like this there was nowhere in the books to hide. Victor, who was an idiot, had either missed the warnings or refused to heed them. It had been months ago that Mike mentioned to him the possibility, and it was going to be just as bad as he thought, if not worse, but at the time Victor just wanted to hear reassurances, nor did he ever check his tactics with Margaret, probably because he did not want to be the bearer of bad news. As for the client, it was not official yet. Margaret had just gotten a phone call from them the other day. With this litany of failure Mike seemed to imply he could only do so much. He was here to record. He was not a decider.

He described a disturbing detail that had come to light; among Rafael's papers Eileen had found a ledger of line-item expenditures, annotations of off-the-books transactions that had been given cover in the official entries she had prepared. With surprising smugness, the quiet, bespectacled girl produced her findings: it was characteristic of Rafael to keep such cleanly delineated memoranda, even if it might seem morbid of him to do so in this case, and it was actually quite common in her experience; cheaters were known to be fastidious. Most of the entries were innocuous and even indicative of the old man's generosity—interest-free loans to employees and the like—while some gave signs of being favors, or bribes, such as to acquire bids. The apartment, though, was the most substantial figure. Notably it was manifested as remittances on payables owed to a "Lena Wu." All titling listed the company as the owner, but it might prove a problem if she produced signed papers claiming they owed her tenancy. So far Eileen had not been able to find a copy of such an agreement, but she had other, circumstantial evidence that she was able to cross-reference in the official ledger, line items for payments made to consultants that had been entered by Rafael himself and later reconciled with other expenses he delivered to Mike and herself for consolidation. It was incontrovertible they were payments and not gifts, and the amounts, once she disentangled them from the consolidated costs, totaled more or less to that of the apartment purchase. There were even references to contractual agreements, but she could not locate these.

My father took all this in without comment at first, but I could tell what he was thinking. It was one thing if, as everyone from the media and the police had it, she had been an inadvertent party to Rafael's death, but this suggested a more active role. Here was evidence supporting what he had always maintained, that the relationship between Lena and Rafael had been transactional, if not verging on extortionate. The media coverage had focused on lascivious details of an extramarital affair that had its origins in conjecture and made Rafael out to be the agent of his own demise; in turn, the perpetrators transmuted into victims, just as they did in Yvonne's book. But if blackmail were involved, with the conspirators perhaps even demanding the company itself, would his death still be pinned on his moral failings? In response to Eileen's report, my father took the opportunity to paint a scene, not one of his friend crazed with jealousy, but instead armed in defense, not just of himself, but his family and employees. When they finished him off, it was not the result they could have hoped for, since he had been the fulcrum of their leverage. Yes, it did seem they had something on him, but if that woman's role were made known, it would shift the tone of conversation around his reputation.

I was asked about the status of the condo. According to the priorities laid out by my father and Mike, its sale had to be quiet; they did not want Margaret knowing of its existence, much less the identity of its tenant. Finding a buyer and turning a profit was not going to be a problem, not in that neighborhood, not with the city flush with nouveau riche paying with literal wads of cash. Instead the trick was going to be coaxing out the tenant, a squatter really, since she was not paying rent and had been relying all this time on our obliviousness. I had suggested Yvonne Fung to handle the sale. We could trust her to smooth things over for what was, in effect, an eviction; we already knew of her discretion and professionalism, but it was her acquaintance with the sensitive background of the occupant, not to mention the occupant herself, that proved unique.

Such secrecy lacked the circular logic of conspiracy and seemed more an act of care. There was a sense of every little thing being overthought, as they often are in family affairs. For instance, Mike had had reservations about Yvonne's suitability for the job. Far from an advantage, having written a book about the very person she was trying to kick out could backfire. Surely Lena must be aware of the novel's existence by now? I did not know, but Yvonne had come to the conclusion she probably had not heard of it, since she was not a book type and a more obscure work of literature would be harder to find. Even if she had, the fact that it was a reimagination of her life would probably not bother her.[18] I did not know how to parse the source of this insight, other than to say we had gotten to know her, myself from reading the novel and Yvonne from writing it.

____

[18] There seems no way around explaining this other than as a footnote: the name of Yvonne's main character, which also forms the basis of her book's title, is a homophone for the name of the real-life woman, who shares the same name as the woman here in my father's account; that is to say, it is composed of different Chinese characters, another reason why the book might not come to her attention.

Their real estate lawyer, Mike said, suggested the safest course of action was to combine a buyout with a new-tenant contract, in order to nullify any possible previous ones; otherwise, the tenant could always cite a verbal agreement between her and her benefactor that we would never be able to disprove.

In all likelihood she would not sign, my father interrupted. His misgivings were of a cultural nature: it was not the way Chinese people did things; we had to appeal to her sense of honor. This was a difficult concept to bring over to the language the trick clauses would be written in, a language that could only speak to either the heart or the mind one at a time and could not conceive of the heart as the same thing as the undivided mind. I thought he was going to add this was no longer a legal matter, that if it was to be tried, it would be in the court of communal opinion. He would propose himself to pronounce collective judgment on her, face-to-face, like a village elder. Would he present the evidence we had laid out before us and appeal to her conscience, to ask her to come clean? Would he threaten to bring this information to the press, to expose her? All of this went beyond the management of the company, and the implications made the three of us, Mike, Eileen, and myself, uneasy. I was about to suggest we bring the matter to Margaret. It was her husband's legacy, after all. In this way we would avoid that responsibility, and she should be the one to call for a renewed investigation of possible criminal acts. My father would not agree, I knew, because he believed he was as much a keeper of that legacy as the widow. It was not Lena Wu who distrusted the law most of all, as it turned out, nor Helen and Victor, but my father. If we were going to take the attorney's advice and bring the renewed lease to the tenant—it was so obviously a trap, he pointed out—who would be able to convince her to sign it?

There were files in LA Eileen still had to go through. The right tack would be to continue to look, Mike suggested, since a confrontation now might risk the tenant going to the landlady on appeal. Until they had hard proof the entries referred to some kind of plot, accusing the tenant would simply pit her word against ours. And if the transaction were something Rafael had entered into willingly, which seemed the case, its legality might be binding. Needless to say, this was sensitive, and highly circumstantial, evidence that should not be discussed beyond this room.

My father noted the occupant should not move without providing forwarding information and that this must be made binding as part of the buyout agreement. The one thing they did not have, though, was time; it was why they were here in the first place, to liquidate assets like the apartment, in order to blunt the cash flow crisis that was upon them. How long could they hold out? They could burn through their reserves for a few months, but if their intention were to shut it all down in the end, they should do it right away.

There was only one possible course of action, my father knew, but before proceeding he wanted Margaret's word. I could imagine why he asked for this; he felt his loyalty had been twisted into something ugly, so that it now only served as a redoubt for his employer. In that room where light did not brighten beyond what filtered through the fog, I could see some of who my father once was, not just to his old friend's wife, but who he had been at the lab and perhaps even when he was still the young scholar. He must have decided not to let this betrayal of his good will go.

They got her on the speakerphone. She would not concur. Her main worry was that it was almost Lunar New Year.

Did the company take days off for New Year, I asked. Did it send people home to their families? No, she replied, they preferred to work, but it was the time of year when her husband used to hand out bonuses.

While everyone waited for my father's response, I checked the calendar on my phone. I had not even noticed it was Chinese New Year. Every year it seemed to get harder to know when it was. Of course in parts of Asia the entire population would be on the move, trying to get back to their hometowns, altering the composition of daily life, but here, nobody knew. The big parade in San Francisco was held, of all things, not on New Year's Day, but two weeks later, during the Lantern Festival. Every year this would confuse me, and I would realize, upon watching footage of the parade on TV, that I had missed the date. I realized this made me out to be a real jook sing, but even in the Bay Area, reminders could be scarce, while of course there were always those who headed out to Chinatown expressly to celebrate it, only to find out that this was the one day, not Thanksgiving or Christmas, that everything was closed. The rare quiet of the alleys on that day would only be broken by intermittent bursts of firecrackers.

In the end my father agreed to make some calls in a last-ditch effort to find a savior. As long as there was a chance, there was no point doing anything irrevocable. On the other hand, it was never a good time for mass firings, and waiting until after the Lantern Festival, if that was the arbitrary moment when a sentimental moratorium should end, would not soften the blow. Of course the very idea of layoffs, even in the case of a single individual, went against Rafael's principles, if any of us truly understood them. Our grasp of those principles, my father commented, seemed to be weakening the more we tried to invoke them.

He laid out his conditions: to spare the staff, Victor and Helen must go, one way or the other, before the new year. They could save themselves a couple of substantial bonuses that way. Herein was the fiscal logic, but everyone knew my father suspected them of being in on the plot, the one in his head, anyway. Mike folded his hands, but Margaret said fine, get it over with, but he should take a plane and do it in person.

To confirm, my father said, it would only be the two of them? Yes, she said, the others could wait, for now. She added that he was to take over their offices. He did not need to be there every day, but he should demonstrate to the staff who was in charge. What about her son? he asked. He was close to Victor, wasn't he? He was not involved, she made clear, so there was no need to consider his point of view.

Music filled the tiny interior of the car. My sister, again. This was not a piece I knew, but I had heard her enough to recognize her expressive quirks. This was not at all like the recent pieces she had sent my father, though. At first it sounded cacophonous to me, which was not atypical, but gradually patterns began to emerge, which was *not* typical. Or was it just my ears, desperate for order, picking them out? Eventually my brain recovered its rhythm; she was playing a ragtime, a genre so unlike anything she usually tackled that I was not prepared to hear it, or what I did hear existed outside of any harmony known to me. I had experienced something like this with languages, when, for instance, one of my parents spoke in English, when I was expecting Mandarin, or vice versa, and I ended up hearing another, garbled tongue. There was also something to her style that made it sound like something else, as if the pieces were being played by a machine, not an electronic synthesizer, but something mechanical.

The ambient light of the ocean-facing side of the Berkeley Hills faded into a purer dark as we emerged out of the tunnel. It had been a late night. With my father's aging eyes, I thought it best to drive him home. Years had passed since I last spent much time here among the quiet and somnolent shadows. I could no longer distinguish where the hill ridges ended and the night sky began, or whether up ahead was the region's only mountain or just black space telescoping out into the delta, toward the Sierras.

My father instructed me to let Lena Wu know we were onto her. I should share what Eileen had uncovered and was also to let him know her reaction. She might or might not agree to what I was to suggest, but there would be no chance with him. I pointed out that it seemed *he* was the one who wanted to talk to her. Didn't he want to hear from her directly what really happened?

He already knew what happened. He had always known. It was just that nobody paid attention to him. He was also pretty sure what she was going to say. It would be nothing of substance. As for whether she would like to hear from him, he paused for a moment, as if considering the possibility, then shook his head. No, he concluded, it was not likely she was ready to listen. I, on the other hand, was around the same age as her and might come across as less threatening.

Of course, he did not want to bring this up in front of Mike and Eileen, whom he felt were being overly concerned with not upsetting Margaret. I should not hold that against them, by the way; they were her employees, after all, in a way we were not. He did not think the tenant would do anything rash, so the odds were the revelation would not get back to them. If that was the case, I asked, then what was the point of doing it? He thought about that for a good minute, while my sister's wild fiddling pinged around the car, and then said he did not know, but once I reported back, the answer would come to him.

Reluctantly I agreed, but I also quietly doubted that confrontation would ever take place, given how elusive the woman was. Only Yvonne had been able to get to her so far, and that had taken some doing. Just my agreeing, and leaving it at that, would be the best-case scenario, I imagined, since I could appease my father while not having to indulge what now seemed like an unhealthy obsession. Over time, as Lena managed to elude me, and I would not try very hard to catch her, his preoccupation would fade and that would be the end of it.

How would I get in touch, he asked. I mentioned I could always just stake out her apartment, but Yvonne Fung seemed the most practical first step. Her again, he grumbled. Had she accepted Ms. Hu's offer yet? Since his work for Margaret made it impossible for him to fulfill his obligations, he had finally been able to convince Ms. Hu to accept his resignation as head of the Society. She then turned to Yvonne, but was still waiting for a reply.

The subject of the Society reminded me of something I had been meaning to ask. I had read his memoir of my sister again. What was the inspiration behind that restaurant scene in Virginia City?

He did not know what I was talking about, since, as he explained, he never looked back at his books once he sent the proofs to the publisher. Of course, now that I had mentioned it, it occurred to him the passage must have been based on all those family trips we used to take to Reno together. There was an air of veracity to that comment; the sections leading up to the scene read like a montage of those trips. I reminded him he had only brought us to Virginia City that one time. His memory apparently stirred, he said that during the course of composition, for the obscure reasons that writers have, he had needed a situation where it was just him and the two of us, away from our mother. So he made it up. He insisted he had never taken us there, not even once. Yes, he was sure of it: that restaurant had been borrowed from a profile in a hotel magazine. He distinctly remembered tearing out the pages to keep as reference.

But I could point to such specific details as the view through the dingy window of the bar, the grain pattern of its wood and the green drapes, not to mention gaps between his account and my recollections, such as the person of the proprietor, who did not make an appearance in real life. Why had he decided to put her there?

I must have gotten it wrong, he said. Maybe I had gone there on my own later on and somehow mixed that trip up with what I read in his book. Since all of us were characters in it, reading it would be much like leafing through old snapshots of yourself, where the photos replaced or got confused with your actual memories, which were hazy at best. It was the reason why he stopped mining his own life for material and also why he never liked taking pictures. At least refraining from both in his old age helped him be surer of himself. His brain may have started to go, but he could be positive about this. As for the character I mentioned, he would have to go back and read the passage again; he did not remember her. (I was sure he would never go back and read it.) Once he did, he was sure he could come up with an explanation. He should know, of all people, shouldn't he? Why didn't I go ask my sister? She would back him up. Because she had never read the book, her memory would not be corrupted by it.

I could already imagine her answer, or rather, the music in the car seemed to be her answer. It had been her way to get away from these questions. I decided to let it go, for now. My father could be stubborn, especially when it came to what he knew or what he thought he knew.

{14}

THE TIME IN THE AIR WAS LESS THAN AN HOUR. I had an eastern-facing view that looked over inland valleys and roads on forested ridges that descended into green foothills dreaming through their hibernation. As those paths narrowed, squeezing between sheer cliffs and the sea, the scale of things grew; in these changes was not just the approach of the dramatic edge of the ocean, the bright surf clinging to mountain-bound strips of coast, the craggy shore and isolated coves gleaming in gradient shades of turquoise, but the sense, generated by the light, that we had entered the south. In fact, we were still to reach the heart of it; the waves were not as stunning a force, and things were calmed by a milder sun and more delicate palm trees that melted into the air. Northern Californians might lump this all into a single stereotype, but in fact this was still the border of a teeming country.

Of that light, there was nothing in the world like it. On the other side of this ocean a more diffuse illumination softened the outline of objects, but here bodies in the afternoon, looking out at the waves, turned into golden sculptures. When the sun set on the surf, objects grew more solid the more infused with light they were, and all of it seemed as if it were about to drop into the waves, which was why, beyond the Greco-Roman trappings, the famous "castle" hereabouts seemed more like a ruin.

The plane began to angle inland, so that now barren gorges stretched out disorientingly in all directions, a much greater wilderness, of chaparral and rock, than anything I had imagined this close to arrival. For a moment I was afraid we had actually caught the wrong flight and passed into Mexico. This would be a much more natural, and less passable, border between the two Californias. It would make more cultural sense if LA were the northern edge of Baja, since its mythology was defined by its inaccessibility, bound by desert, ocean, and this often unremarked stretch of brutal terrain. That it was a kind of inverse and microcosm of the rest of the United States was rooted in its remoteness. In another shift, the endless grid of the San Fernando Valley, mute in shades of earth but accented by jewellike swimming pools, filled the entire window.

Once we landed, the three of us, which included Eileen, but not Mike, picked up our rental car and headed out, with me behind the wheel, down long, palm-lined avenues, away from the ocean. The road seemed to be moving by us while we stayed fixed in place, the light dying, but still warm. Part of me wished we had driven the whole way, as I disliked flying even over short distances, one of the reasons, my sister speculated, I never left the Bay Area. We were not able to take our time coming here, though, not with Margaret and Mike egging us on. Apparently the employment attorney Mike consulted had taken the opposite view, warning him we had not taken sufficient precautions and should build in another two weeks to get our documents in order. That would have put us past the new year, though, which was not to be contemplated, and anyway in our hearts we knew Helen and Victor would never resort to legal action, because they put no stock in the law. If they had something to settle with us, they would do so honorably, if vindictively.

Chinese words, the much-misunderstood logographs so beloved by Rafael, appeared in greater profusion the deeper inland we drove. Who, I began to wonder, lived in the south? If the north possessed a faded cultural glamor to a dated émigré imagination such as Ms. Hu's, who without question chose San Francisco for the headquarters of the Society, newer immigrants, Cantonese, Taiwanese, or mainlander, had no such capital-in-exile to call their own, the way they did in, say, Koreatown or Westminster. Those Chinese immigrants were only here to get themselves mixed up, having just been thrown together, none of them really knowing what went on in their own places. And yet had not Uncle Rafael established his base here, instead of closer to home? Empires, the majesties of Arcadia and Rowland Heights, had been built.

Once, my family had a chance to move to San Diego, thanks to a job offer my father received. He had only received two such invitations in his life. The first came when he found himself at the end of his rope in Salt Lake City, isolated and on the verge of going back to Taiwan in disgrace, or to disgrace; that would have been the outcome, but for an unexpected call from an old teacher to join him in Berkeley, a path that led directly to the lab and continued without turn or surprise to the present day. This all seemed part of the preordained gauntlet of tests and research he had been on since childhood, but the second offer presented a detour. It was my mother who kept things on course, her excuse being that both my sister and I had just entered school; a more truthful explanation was that she was simply one of those people who resisted things for the sake of resisting them. How she had managed to convince herself to study abroad, and eventually settle in the US with my father, was something I never quite understood.

Somewhere along Wilshire the charred odor of fresh asphalt mingled into the soupy air, and it reminded me of something it took me a while to recognize: a section from Yvonne's novel, of Lena's last days in Los Angeles. The passage came back to me because I seemed to be in it now, and it had stood out because the use of hallucination was atypical of the rest of the book and uncharacteristic of Yvonne's work as a whole; there was a mysticism that suggested madness, which was perhaps intentional, and the overall effect was as if a dream had been inserted into a documentary. There was also something insincere about its abrupt climax. It seemed the result of a careless editor requesting a pivotal event to occur, in order to drive the character development, since the actual events, which after all Yvonne was more or less tied to, offered none.

The map grew bigger. Since Rafael set up the condo in San Francisco for her, he had been hinting she make the move permanent. At the same time, the casino had upgraded her hourly rate and was sending more shifts her way. Things were looking up. The drives through the desert, as much as she enjoyed them, day or night, began to feel impractical. She could not sustain the distances for long. San Francisco, Los Angeles, and Las Vegas, at least one of the points in that triangle had to give. From a short-term financial view, that would seem to be LA, since there was no present or future business keeping her there and Lincoln was now no longer an excuse, but she could not see herself cashing in her chips, so to speak, and setting up shop elsewhere, as Rafael suggested. The points of that geometry seemed only to grow further apart, the distances stretching until it was not only those lines that would snap.

In the desert she could hear voices, not the ones in her head, which she came to recognize as not her own, but others' that echoed there. The ones in the desert, although external, spoke directly to her, without being patronizing. They revived the silenced voices in her head and encouraged them to speak again. How long had it been? All that existed now existed in this present time, but she did not find that a problem. Instead it turned her toward her inner ear, where it converged with her vision, because the desert did not just contain voices, but wrote letters in the shapes of mystery-laden rocks, desiccated plant life, and landforms patterned by flows no longer extant.

The city began to appear in bits and pieces in the sand, then completely overtook it. She peered down one of the long boulevards that eventually led to the ocean, when the earth opened up beneath her. Being from Taiwan, she was not new to such things, but this was her first one here. For a moment, she wondered if it was just the car hitting a bump in the road. Or was it her psychic state? If it was, what might come out of it but energy, not in the form of steam or petroleum bubbling out of the ground, but forces of her mind?[19]

---

[19] From *The Lost Lives of Lena Wu.*

I saw the pylon sign I was looking for on the horizon and changed lanes, preparing to turn into the strip-mall parking lot that was our destination, when my phone pinged. Thinking it was Yvonne, since I had just been thinking of her, I pulled over to the curb, but when I checked my phone, I found a text message from my sister. She had been carrying twins. She and her husband had not wanted to know the sex of the babies, which annoyed my mother (my father less so). In the picture she sent, she was sitting and smiling in bed wearing a hospital gown, with two newborns, in standard-issue pink-and-blue-striped knit caps, shriveled and bundled things indistinguishable from each other. The accompanying message pointed out which was the girl and which was the boy.

No one received us, but it did not take long to be recognized and let in. It was still morning, and everyone already seemed lost in work, in both senses of the word, of being deep into work, which was admirable, and being lost, for they did not know their future. Despite their silence, we could sense fear. The plant appeared to be fully staffed, with the only notable missing people Victor and Helen themselves.

In the break room, my father helped himself to the stash of bottled water and made himself comfortable. I joined him there, while Eileen slipped into the archives. Her clandestine task, to rifle through Rafael's archives for clues to his private life that had been disguised as financial records, was different from ours, but we decided having her come with us would be the best way to keep her unnoticed.

As we waited, Eileen did not emerge, and by noon the

interim general managers had not showed. My father called over one of the technicians, someone he had a passing acquaintance with, and sent him over to their house to report back. Then he called the employment attorney, who suggested we send over the papers by courier, with a notary. That would be the smart move, but after hanging up, my father decided, given the unexpected developments so far, one or both of us should be there to make sure things were done right.

We got into our rental car again and lost our way immediately. According to the map, it was not far by Southern Californian standards, but trying to cut through the sprawling neighborhoods, viaducts, and uneven terrain northeast of downtown, instead of overshooting and backtracking on the freeway, was a mistake. For us, being out-of-towners, it was especially confusing; it was not clear if their house was in the "city" or the "valley," that is, on which side of the hills it was. I circled some very narrow, steep, residential-looking streets of older homes, which resembled the mazey vertical neighborhoods typical of San Francisco; the giveaway here were the front yards planted with cacti. As we climbed and approached the cloudless sky, the sun's heat pressed stronger against our little car. At a certain point, the street went as high as it could go; where one would expect to flip over the ridge and begin the descent, we were instead cut off by a cul-de-sac ending in a wire-fenced lot, the edge of the world.

I texted the technician in case the notary arrived before we did, but he did not reply. Instead my father called the plant and was told our emissary had returned along with Helen and Victor. They had been briefed that we were looking for them and were trying to get in contact with us. (On top of everything else, the area we had been driving in had poor cell phone coverage.) While we were waiting to get a report on them, they apparently had been getting a report on us.

On the way back to the plant, my father filled me in. For the past few months, Helen had been taking staffers, even temps, into her confidence, telling them a sale was imminent and that she had been promised an executive position. Of course it did not take long for word to spread as intended, and by this method she cultivated loyalties, undermining my father's authority even before he had begun to impose it. She did nothing to hide her behavior, and my father took this as a warning to him, and through him to Margaret, that any deal brokered by us would be perceived as hostile and set off a revolt. She had thus positioned herself and her husband as the ones out to save the company's jobs, while we were the ones to eliminate them. Speculation was swirling, and with our arrival, the day seemed at hand.

He did not rule out the possibility that Margaret herself had been the source of the rumors. That made no sense, I said, considering we had been sent by her to fire Victor and Helen. Why prop them up, even surreptitiously, only to undermine them down the road? He did not say I was naïve, as I suppose I was too old for that. In their *community*, he explained, reputation mattered more than anything, even money. It was why, for instance, he had been so insistent on clearing Rafael's name. In such circumstances, it was often necessary to please everybody, but since of course that was not possible, at least the perception that one was trying was just as important. For Margaret, this meant bringing my father on, so she would be seen to be doing the right thing by those waiting for her to abide by her husband's judgment. At the same time, she needed to be seen as making the attempt, at least, to protect her workers. Helen and Victor were expendable; they commanded no true loyalty from their charges. Her ultimate purpose was to place her son in a good position. It was an obligation I might not understand.

When we arrived at the plant, we were surprised to find it empty. There was only the technician there, who had been told to wait for us.

Would we be present for the lunch? he asked.

What lunch?

The entire company had been invited.

By whom?

The young master, who was going to be there. Helen had made the announcement.

What was this all about?

Didn't we know? They all thought that was why we were here. They were frightened, to say the least. Why hadn't Margaret been by for so long?

Everyone would be assembled by the time we got there. The location was right next door, inside the restaurant connected to the underground garage. We had to go downstairs, then take the elevator back into the banquet hall.

The technician escorted us. We were directed to one of the tables furthest from the dais by another employee whom my father had been on good terms with, but who now regarded him suspiciously. Before us stretched a tableau that seemed one of those that reverberated through history, populated by would-be emperors and warlords who had been invited to feasts only to meet their ends at them. Ten round tables took up the hall, with Helen, Victor, and Rafael's son enthroned at the end of the long room, joined by an older man whom neither of us recognized. Cabbage-colored drapes covered the windows. The only hint of the midday LA glow came through the skylights, and behind Helen hung an embroidered tapestry of a phoenix, which in Chinese culture was not a symbol of rebirth, although in this case I thought Helen would not mind the misinterpretation, since she seemed the kind of person taken in by that kind of sort of symbolism. Based on the number of tables and my knowledge of the company head count (the precise figure would have weighed heavily on my father's mind), the banquet hall, booked, I imagined, at no small cost, fit the entire staff exactly. Maybe there were some people on sick leave or traveling; no one that I saw gave off the air of being a spouse or a guest, unless those spouses also worked for the firm. This probably only applied to Victor and Helen. Eileen was nowhere to be found. I imagined her ducking into a row of file cabinets when they were rounding up everyone for lunch.

By the time we sat down, the cold starters, jellyfish salad and spiced pork slices, had already been picked through, but the main dishes were still on their way. It would probably be something with its head still on, a fish or a bird, to indicate new beginnings.

Helen and Victor sat there with the confident look of survivors. What did they know? What did they *think* they knew? The cost of holding this pageant had perhaps not occurred to them, nor the lost productivity. A new frugality would apparently not be the theme of the day, or if it was, they were certainly sending the wrong message. Instead, in keeping with this banquet, they presented themselves as the bringers of good tidings, and the crowd must have picked up on this. For all their apprehension, there was a certain giddiness in the air: a relief perched on the precipice, since at the very least, the waiting was about to be over. Despite Margaret's backing, my father was becoming convinced, or was convincing himself, that she was the one who put her son up to the whole circus. Had she executed a deal? If she had, her son would not say anything to his face, but would instead work on my father behind the scenes. The final blow would arrive long before he even suspected it. And by not taking sides, or rather by taking all sides, she with some patience could allow the best solution to emerge. According to him, as he almost muttered under his breath, to no one in particular, it was the way she managed Rafael, too, until her passivity led to tragedy; he said this in a way that insinuated she was responsible for what had happened.

No doubt, I imagined, Victor and Helen's forthcoming firings would come as a shock to everyone, but I believed a wave of relief would pass over them as they realized no one else was affected and perhaps even dared to entertain a glimmer of hope that this might be all there was to it. My father's bet on the two of them not being much liked would be right on: Margaret would have her new year's reprieve, and he, on the other hand, would have won some measure of satisfaction on Rafael's behalf. Mike would also be right that the financial fallout, which ostensibly this was all about, would not be mitigated. The trimming might help prepare for a sale, but without more, they would find themselves in the same situation in which they started. Rafael would never have agreed to sell his business. In essence his work had been to prepare it for his son, and faced with the same choices, he would have gone down with the ship. My father knew that, but in the end he agreed to find a buyer, perhaps because he had never had his principles tested or because his mind had been honed all those years to optimize outcomes. To me, his suspicions of Margaret, as with all his judgements when it came to Rafael, seemed unwarranted. If this purchase were to be introduced through the excommunicated Victor, would she even bother to entertain it? Hadn't she promised my father, if a bit wearily, that her son would report to him in the new organization? The boy would not like it, but he would not have a choice.

Probably because he had been so caught up in the proceedings, and his attempts to read into them, my father did not pay attention to the food being served and ate absent-mindedly, something I took notice of as the pile of crab shells grew steadily on his plate. Mango pudding in cubes of almond jelly arrived as Victor took the microphone to announce the company's bailout. Rafael's son, pasty-faced under greasy black-red hair, maintained a fixed, slightly haughty expression. In the now stuffy hall, the circumspect guests, mindful of any gesture that might be taken the wrong way, politely applauded the man from Shanghai, who was named Li. He went on to give a brief eulogy in memory of Rafael, whom he claimed as an old friend.

The mood in the room improved. Everyone was just happy to know they would be returning to their desks that afternoon and the luncheon was not what they had feared. All they had to do for now was to hear out the vaguely longer-term vision laid out by their would-be leaders. Surrounded by their "key people," Helen, Victor, and Rafael's son struck statuesque poses. It was not clear if the latter knew his mother had already signed the papers for the former two's dismissal.

As the so-called investor made the rounds and began to shamble toward us, I stepped outside to check my phone. It was good to be away from that claustrophobic atmosphere, but standing on the exposed sidewalk, under the afternoon sun, did not feel much better. Before long, Rafael's son joined me. He introduced himself and told me he recognized me from his father's funeral. He knew about Yvonne's book, the one that sought to exonerate his father's murderer. The author had approached his mother for an interview a little more than a year ago. At the time, he took her as an ally, but now he saw his mother was right to reject her advances. I should not think his mother did not hear of the book's publication, he said. They were now considering legal action. He wanted me to know that. I pointed out it was a work of fiction, as far as I knew. I had not read it myself. Nor had he, he admitted, but Victor had told him everything. Now he understood how my father was taking advantage of his family's tragedy, putting himself in position to take over the company. I reminded him it was his mother who decided that. Our fathers were friends; more than that, my father had always respected the way his did things and tried to follow his example. He was only stepping into this role because he thought that was what Uncle Rafael would have wanted, and it had been the same with Yvonne. It was unfortunate. Having her report the case should have exposed the truth, but instead she chose to fabricate the story, focusing on a character she made up called Lena Wu, from what I had heard, rather than writing a work of properly researched journalism. Worse, in my opinion, was that she blended facts with fiction, coming up with something that was neither.

That was why he and Victor had taken the sale of the company into their own hands. How many offers did I think his mother could collect? She was no businesswoman, and neither was my father. Every decision they had made so far had backfired. He told me he did not want to see me again. As for my father, they would deal with him after the sale was completed. I told him I was sorry he felt that way. He went back inside. Based on his remarks, I assumed he did not know about the notary, who texted me saying she was underground looking for a parking spot and would be there in a few minutes with papers for Victor and Helen to sign.

{15}

YVONNE PEERED UP FROM HER CARDBOARD COFFEE CUP.

"I would have loved to see the look on his face when the notary showed up," she said. "Your father fired them on the spot, in front of the entire company, I hope."

Of course not, I said. It was done discreetly. When the notary called, I gave her directions to the plant, and we met with them in their office. My father did not get the justice he craved, or if he did, it was cold justice that only managed to fulfill his duty to Rafael. Far from any measure of satisfaction, he found it, he later confessed, one of the saddest moments of his life. Helen and Victor had not expected it, to say the least, and the force of it must have been multiplied coming on the heels of their moment of triumph. It made me think my father had been wrong to suspect them of conspiring against his old friend; they seemed puzzled why he and Margaret would do this, when they were only carrying out what they believed to be their boss's wishes. As for my father, he had been stoic through his delivery of the spiel he had been instructed to give, but once the pair left the room, he broke down. I could not see how he could do this to the entire company, but maybe such tasks came easier in bunches.

As for Rafael's son, in fact I did not get to see the look on his face. He disappeared when I went back into the restaurant and did not show up again. Maybe he knew what was coming.

Yvonne got up. It was one of those afternoons when the fog, roused by the wind, emerged from its oceanic sleep; the view outside her picture window became a shifting pattern of white-on-white in attenuated light, even though it was still midday. In an attempt to keep us warm, she brewed a couple of cups of coffee in an old, streak-stained drip machine she kept on top of a filing cabinet, and brought two cups over, hers doused with milk, mine black.

After our last conversation, she had gone back and read my father's memoir. Of course she regretted she had not earlier. It was a better book than any of hers, she admitted with false modesty. At the same time, it contained no surprises; it was an artless reflection of the man we both knew. As for the scene I had mentioned, she paid particular close attention to it and concurred the resonances were eerie. Attributing the similar characters and identical locations to coincidence, not to mention the placement of both scenes near the ends of their respective books, only made it all stranger. It made her think, just who was this person she was dealing with? Given the passage of time, the woman in my father's book could not be the one in hers. Lena, however, was real, she insisted. I would find out soon enough. She showed me an open tab on her phone, in case I doubted: a message she had just sent asking to arrange a meeting. What would I do once I met her, face-to-face?

I did not know what I would *say* to her when we met, but I would *show* her what we had against her, as I promised my father I would.

"How dutiful of you," Yvonne said.

I imagined Margaret reading Yvonne's book: bits and pieces of it ricocheting through her mind as she turned its pages, familiar names and events redolent of real memories. If Lena was real, it was also obvious in her book she was simply Yvonne's younger self. I knew this even though I had always been skeptical when writers spoke of turning into their own characters, as if possessed. I was never one of those readers who considered every character in every book to be merely some aspect of their author's own personality. But here, what seemed to be happening was some measure of autonomy for both. The characters were shrapnel of the observed world that, once embedded in the writer's psyche, became colored by it, so that one became infused with the other. In my father's case, even with something as straightforward as a portrait of his own daughter, a book made of meticulously drawn scenes of daily life, there were still many details, beyond the ones recorded, that needed to be supplied by the author's imagination. In this way, my sister's childhood became my father's childhood, not the other way around. I supposed some people might work differently, but how far do we know anybody, really? For example, did Rafael have it in himself to be a murderer? It seemed an alien narrative had invaded his person, which in turn was transformed by latent frustrations, not merely jealousy, which alone could not, I surmised, account for as overdetermined an act as attempted murder. No, some greater outrage was involved.

One difference, I observed, was that Lena had arrived in America earlier in her life than Yvonne had. Perhaps for that reason she was better able to take full advantage of it. Picture her, I said, having grown up in parochial, smog-ridden Taipei, now in a California beach town, looking out on the waves. Yvonne said she was well acquainted with this kind of person. They were every one of her potential new homeowners. Their investments, once made, would only keep metastasizing in value. Something Yvonne once said to me about her real estate investment philosophy, when we were in the car on that road trip together, seemed to apply: "My strategy is very simple. Never lose money." It struck me as the opposite of optimism. Perhaps what Yvonne was projecting onto this younger woman was not her own decision to come to America, but her earlier decision to go to China. What lay behind it? She may not have known herself. She did not talk about that part in her book; every story was a scenario that took place after the protagonist got there. Those currents that drove her to the mainland, at that moment of upheaval, would have been much like the currents that drove someone like Lena to America today, that is, to destroy everything.

There were truths Yvonne could not get into the introduction to her book, but perhaps she had dealt with them, however obliquely, in the body of it, in the portrait of her elusive protagonist.

We always thought Americans lived in the future, she said, with its frontier and technology, but once we got here, all we saw was their past. Maybe it was not so apparent to themselves, but it was nakedly obvious to the newcomer that America was nothing but bygone customs, dragged across the continent. It was their houses, which were hardly ever razed and rebuilt, but instead reinhabited, over and over. As immigrants we were told our every move would be a re-creation of our heritage, but was there a single traditional thing we ever did? Instead everything we made was from whatever was at hand.

Did I think of Lena as a traditional Chinese woman? Because she wanted money? Let's say she ran a laundry or a restaurant, somewhere in Chinatown or Stockton, the kind of humble business the Chinese had been running here for generations. Did that make her traditional? The old country had moved on too, so we never went forward and never went back. We did not reinvent. We just started over again and again. There was something unreal about people who did just what they set out to do, with no obligation to the past or the future. Everything in this country was understood backward; the more recent the arrival, the more American, the truly exceptional.

This had always held true, she believed, until the latest generation; it seemed they had faded away. For herself, what might be achieved lay right before her. If she were dissatisfied, and who was not, it was with other people, or the world, but never herself. When she looked at Rafael, she saw the same thing. This woman, on the other hand, was killing herself from inside, envious, unable to bring herself to take, and overreaching when she finally tried. She went through all the motions but the important ones. It was not simply a matter of settling for more or for less. She wanted less. From her observations of Lena, it seemed there was something that she could not quite put her finger on, that made her subtly more real and therefore just ordinary, one ghost among many, the created instead of the creator. I said it sounded as if Yvonne knew her pretty well, maybe even better than I had thought. What did I think about my parents, she asked. Were they like herself? I saw them in a certain light, I said, but I would not say I really knew them.

{16}

My sister said she wanted to go swimming. It had been so hot lately my mother said she would not mind taking a dive herself, but my father had not cleaned the pool for weeks. Was it all right for her to go into the water so soon? Of course it was, my sister said. It was her regular exercise. No one did the postpartum month anymore, resting in bed and drinking bitter boiled medicine to replace the body's vital energies. The American doctors pushed her out of the hospital the day after the kids were born and encouraged her to go bike riding and take mountain hikes, much to my mother's chagrin. My father did not know about swimming, but as a man of science, he was okay with it if the doctors were. He got up and inserted the brush into the end of the long aluminum pole that could reach the deep end of the pool; the robot sweeper, pushed along by water pumped through its tentacles, glided past his scrubbing.

Beyond him, in the foothills, watered lawns and topiary preserved the illusion of eternal spring, but at higher elevations, on either side of the valley, the irrigation no longer flowed, leaving the hillsides open to the sun and its wild vegetation to hold its own, prickly and close to the ground. The sound of cheers from a Little League game rose over the backyard fence, more ghostly than it should have been, given the proximity.

The babies were still formless, pure distillations of life. Even so, I thought I could discern their separate destinies, although I could not tell which was the boy and which was the girl. In voodoo, didn't the world begin with a pair of twins? They were physically identical, squirming in their respective car seats, which could reattach to their dual stroller. Did I really not know? my sister asked. Our mother could tell them apart. She picked one of them out of its uncomfortable-looking seat, stepped off the deck built from two-by-fours by our father, and headed to the pergola, also hand-built by him, where she held the newborn out in the hot sun. It blinked at the sunlight as if it were a solid thing, even trying to grab it. I enjoyed the sense of vicariously seeing the world for the first time; it was only through the eyes of an infant that viewing the world anew did not seem like some sort of self-deceiving trick.

They were here for the red-egg ceremony, stopping by before heading to Southern California for my brother-in-law's job interview. My mother did not think they should have flown out with the babies only a month old, but my sister said she was going stir crazy at home and insisted on coming along. If her husband got the position, our parents could see their grandchildren more often, especially since my father worked in LA. Actually he would not go that often, my father said, in his deflating manner. They did not like him much; he would probably be fired soon, if one could be fired from working on a volunteer basis. He added this last point with a clownish grin, but no one was laughing. If he did take the job and they made the move, what would my sister do? What about her job? Well, she sighed, to tell the truth, she had been thinking about giving up teaching and taking some time off. It was not a secure position, and they were dumping classes and administrative work on her. This was all news to my mother, who, despite finding fault with all else she did, had been under the impression my sister was an academic star. Her husband backed up her sad testimony, adding she would not be missing anything. He had done the same thing when he was her age, at the same stage of his career, that is, quitting his job and taking the opportunity to devote to personal projects, a precious and magical time, before returning to academia. He encouraged her to take the chance, but maybe it was tougher to get back into the job market nowadays. There was no doubt about it, my father commented gloomily, every-thing was tougher.

One of the babies started screaming. Maybe a fly landed on its head. Whatever it was, it got the other one going. Crying was expected, of course, but what happened next was remark-able. I had thought both parents would run over to calm them, but only their father did; my sister, on the other hand, went to her violin case. They had recently found a sure-fire way to put the twins to sleep, she explained while tightening the strings of her bow. Her husband put both babies into their car seats, then clicked them into the stroller. With a look and a nod, the kind that would be exchanged between two players in a duet, my sister began to bow, while my brother-in-law rocked the children in their stroller. It did not work with just any piece of music, she told me, in a soft voice. Only this one. What made the whole display more bizarre was the music was not a lullaby; it was not even music to my ears, but a series of drones and squeals. Once the babies fell asleep, she abruptly stopped playing.

The work was based on piano rolls, she explained, leaving the twins on the deck as we went into the house, so we could speak without keeping our voices down. It was while practicing and reshaping the piece, smoothing out the arpeggios into drones, that she stumbled upon its soporific effect on her children, and what had interested her about it was not so much the changes in timbre moving from player piano to strings, so much as the transposition of hearing the music played by machine to hearing it by a human being, how, in interpretation, she emulated the machine: to play not as she had been trained to do, with expression, but the flat consistency of the mechanical. On the other hand, when she studied her first player piano, she was surprised at how visceral it looked from the inside, with its gears laid bare. She could see its humanity. If she had more time, and was not burdened by the babies, she would have liked to have gone to the Musée Mécanique. She had never been there before and only learned about it from her research.

But she had gone there, I reminded her. We went together, as children. Maybe she had forgotten because back then it was still by Ocean Beach. I described to her the miragelike view of the sunken ship from Land's End and the peepshow machines, antique panoramas, and laughing automatons, in addition to the self-playing pianos, but she had no memory of any of them. I must have gone alone, she said. Her reply reminded me of what I had been meaning to ask her about Virginia City.

Did she remember *that*? It was the two of us with our father, our mother having chosen to stay behind at the hotel in Reno. There was the main street, something straight out of an old Western, and the Chinese restaurant with its strange proprietress. No, she was sorry, maybe all of those things did happen, but childbirth and raising two newborns may have given her partial amnesia, she said only half jokingly.

I believed her when she said she had not been there. Had *I*? There had been the player piano at Tao House, but it could not have been confused with the ones I saw at Ocean Beach. Despite my recollection of details as fixed as the words on this page, this was when I began to feel the ground shift, as it had for Lena. The chance of my sister suffering from some kind of memory erasure caused by childbirth seemed less likely than my recalling events that had never occurred. The sense of never being the same person as the one I was a moment ago was not unfamiliar.

Over lunch, my sister asked my father if she could have a copy of the book he wrote about her. An academic couple, friends of hers, were interested in translating it. How they learned of it was pure coincidence. The wife, who was from Taiwan, had read the serialized installments when they came out every week, and once they were introduced, she put two and two together. As a former violinist and child prodigy herself, she had been left with a deep impression of my sister's upbringing, but had never been able to track down the finished book. Now here she was speaking with the grown-up version of its subject. Although she had proposed translating my father's memoir simply so my sister and her husband could read it, her husband, an executive at a university press, found the premise fascinating; perhaps he could even help get it published. Would my father be open to having it translated and shown to an editor?

My father did not think that would be a good idea. He looked at my sister and then at her husband, as if trying to pry some insight from her rarefied world. What went through their heads out there? At the laboratory, they were intellectuals and isolated in their own way too, but at least they knew they were part of something greater, by means of subterranean, indeed subatomic, channels.

For him, my sister's marriage somehow transformed her from a daughter into a peer, and instead of gaining a son, he found himself talking to a man not much younger than himself. When they were first getting to know each other, her husband had seemed standoffish, but eventually my father grew used to the silences, understanding he was not shy, nor was there, as might be commonly supposed, a cultural or linguistic gap. The fellow was just always listening, as befit a musician. He was, in other words, an eccentric; my sister would pick that type.

Over the years, whether she was conscious of his sense of distance toward her and her husband or not, she made subtle accommodations, but during her pregnancy she changed into something that was not a coherent personality, but a state. Now she had transformed yet again. It was not quite a reversion, although some trace of her former self had come out of hiding. She was not the girl my father still thought of when he thought of her, but something intermediate: a mature woman.

Before he could elaborate his objections, I found myself suddenly present and, without forethought, cut in. "You should let them do it." Having an English translation released by a legitimate American publisher would give the Society something to talk about. That would make Ms. Hu happy, and an announcement of a translation, from no matter how minor a press, would come off well.

He got up from the table, the same one my sister and I had eaten at since we were children, and walked over to the bookshelf. He pulled out a copy of the memoir and handed it to her. She said she would have the translation sent over as soon as it was completed, for his approval. That would not be necessary, he replied, since he did not feel qualified to judge. Instead she should have it sent to me. I agreed to review it for publication.

After my sister's swim, my mother told her to wait for her hair to dry before hitting the road, since she might catch a cold, but my sister laughed it off. It was late afternoon, and they would not arrive in Santa Barbara until night. For two people who paid so much attention to time, as the structural basis of their art, they managed it terribly.

Each of them took up one baby in its seat and carried it, swinging from their elbows. Once the kids were strapped in, my brother-in-law brought out the luggage, the breast-pump contraption slung over one shoulder by a strap, the diaper bag over the other. My sister said goodbye. We were not sure when we would see each other again. Of course we did not know it then, but it would not be until my father's funeral.

Their blue rental car backed into the end of the cul-de-sac. Through the side window, they waved at my parents and me as we waved back from the top of the driveway.

{17}

EVEN IF LEGALLY IT WAS NOT HERS AND MORE LIKE MINE (at least that was how my argument would go), insofar as I was its owner's representative, she did not invite me into her home. It made sense she would want to meet somewhere discreet, yet public, where I could not make a scene. Tucked in this unheralded corner of the city, the restaurant lay closer to my home than hers, although I had never been here before. The chef was famous, she explained, having won a Michelin star for another, more pretentious establishment, so although we were only having sandwiches, they came with a pedigree.

At the same time, she was in no mood to go on about herself, if she ever was. Instead she resorted to an old tactic of concealment, turning the focus of the conversation on the other party, namely myself. Where did I see this all going? she asked. She could not imagine me working for Margaret or the new owners after they acquired the business; I was meant for a better fate. Supporting my father was one thing, but he was already retired now. It was time for me to consider my own place in the world. Nor would it be, she believed, with the Society.

Literature was a strange game to her. It had no rules and no discernible outcomes.

She ate her sandwich, in real time, not literary time. Not only was she no longer the character I had read about in Yvonne's book, she was already moving away from whoever she was now. Time had been rendered visible, not by our situation, but in a willed way; she palpably had plans to be elsewhere. This was a noticeable quality of hers, as I should have recalled.

What was her aspiration? I had not anticipated to see her for who she was, in the undeniability of her presence, when there had been so much mythology woven around her. I had not expected that to be so easily cut away. I saw her urge to exist in the present tense, rather than a disassociated past or future, or an imaginary alternate, a continuous effort she exerted against forces that would otherwise make her into something else. To be unknown was her means of continuation. Obscurity was her protection. Perversely, it was this incongruity with the various stories swirling around her that made her, in her real life, a superior literary character, a figment of writers' imaginations contained by no single book. Despite the fact that she had no aspirations to be anything other than who she was at any given moment, a welcome trait that did not belong to almost everybody else around me, she had become a fictional person.

She was not being forthcoming and barely bothered to hide it. Unsurprisingly she came across as a composite of what everyone had made her out to be: my father's brainchild, but also Yvonne's, who had elaborated her myth, more deftly than I had first thought, by drawing the threads of rumor, testimony, reportage, and her own words into a consistency. That consistency made her less successful as a literary character in the fiction she starred in than the one sitting before me, consistency being the quality we look for in real people, not literature, a product of our tendency to turn even those we know best into cardboard cutouts.

So she was who she really was, the younger Yvonne, decked out in a matching carrot-orange jogging outfit that was probably quite expensive, set off by flashes of garish accessories.

I had the paper drafted by our lawyer that would nullify any previous agreement about the apartment, written or verbal, folded on the table, next to my sandwich plate.

"I'm not going to walk away from money, but keep in mind people like you and me aren't so easy to get rid of."

Why bring me into it? Of course she would not walk away on the spot. At least she had to consider our offer. The agreement came out to subsidizing one year of her rent, whether or not she chose to stay.

"You plan to move out, all the same?"

"Maybe." She grabbed the paper and began to skim it. "Maybe not. You want me to leave?"

"My job's to make sure the past is covered. We're selling the place, so the future's someone else's problem. But I think the buyer prefers you stay."

"Who's they?"

"A family trust. They're looking at this as an income property. So it could work out for you. At the same time, I guess it'd be easy enough for them to find a new tenant."

"Yes, we're all replaceable."

She stuffed the paper into her purse.

"You're going to think it over?"

"You think I'm going to sign it right here?"

"Do you have any prior agreements with Rafael about the place?"

"If I sign it, it wouldn't really matter, now would it?"

I wanted to do my duty, ask how she had gotten where she did and how she had dragged Rafael there. I brought up the records Elaine had disinterred, their hints at agreements with, or concessions from, Rafael. Her response this time, stating without ambiguity there was no such arrangement, suggested she was calling my bluff. Rafael had simply allowed her to live there and gave her the keys. After his death, she still had them, and nobody had come to take them away. If I did not believe her, how about if she signed the papers right now? She brought them back out and held a pen over them. Well? This was what I wanted wasn't it? I stuck to my plan and said that one way or the other, we would sell the place. She would have to face the new landlords on their terms, with whatever protection she had. Which she chose was not our concern. She smiled knowingly and scribbled her name down, then turned the papers around and pushed them, grease stained and covered in crumbs, across the table.

I had not thought she would sign, or if I did, it would have only been after a tortuous wait. I imagined she would have milked the suspense, while the situation unraveled or chance brought new combinations into play. I thought she would only show her cards when the new owners came for her, driving up the price of her departure in the process. Wasn't that how business was done? Instead she had given up the greater value, without leveraging her advantage, time. It was as if she were impulse-buying her innocence, which I had not expected would be so valuable to her. She had withstood the rumormongering so far. Why make that sacrifice now? Perhaps that apartment had not only been a means to hide in plain sight, but a trap, laid by Rafael, and we had presented her the means to escape.

Was I to let it go at that? I must admit that I faltered at this point, as my father knew I would. The confession or act of contrition he had ordered I extract from her would not be forthcoming. I could only say to him that she did not bother to hide her guilt. We would let her walk off with our money, knowing what she had done to Uncle Rafael. What else could we do? Despite what my father believed, we did not have the power to prosecute. In the end all we had was the community mind; she was a marked woman in the eyes of those people, and perhaps that was enough. Rafael's widow did not know it, but at least she would be freed of her specter now. I was fully aware this all sounded like a rationalization for my failure to shame Lena further.

Walking back to her car, she wanted to stop by the art complex next door, where according to her an unusual auction had been held. Outside the sun was bright but cold, a typical combination for the city. In the transition from the interior of the restaurant, the windblown streets took on the character of a small port town. The auction was held right next door, she said. Billionaires were something this city was not lacking. It strained credulity to think a masterpiece by the greatest artist in the history of the world would sit without fanfare behind the aluminum siding of this neighborhood of moldering warehouses, but that was also keeping with the character of this city, which stowed its illuminations in fogbound blocks of begrimed concrete behind unprepossessing doorways.

She said my parents lived in a very proscribed world and accused me of having developed a derivative conception of myself, in which I had chosen not to become one of those second-generations who went off to "realize themselves." I knew what she meant, right? When the Cantonese said *jook sing,* they got it wrong. The ABCs were solid, not hollow. They were no different than any other American. People like my parents were the ones who were disconnected, but for whatever reason, I chose to live in their empty world. She respected that. I grew up here, but she liked to think we were alike. She knew this was our first time to meet, but the two of us had been through this whole story together. Who created this situation? Rafael, my father, Yvonne. We were lucky, because we were irrelevant and undetected, while the world, and money, flowed to us. For so many people, what they fought for just did not come to them, but if we situated ourselves correctly, it would of its own accord. She used to have this argument with Rafael all the time. What were you looking to get out of this? she asked him. He did not need to serve the company. The company should serve him.

Was I right to hear she saw something of herself in me? As reluctant protagonists of stories imagined by others, we were compatriots; I could not tell if in pointing this out she was being manipulative. I did not see myself that way at all.

When I started compiling this—what was this exactly? a memoir? a journal? a transcription?—I thought I would be supporting my father by explaining his motives, but instead I seemed to have only succeeded in discrediting them.

"The lesson I learned was it's better for me to work alone," she said.

"You really have thought this through."

"I've had the opportunity to do that. From the trail you've left, I can tell you have brains, although it's not exactly clear in what way. No offense, but you don't strike me as anybody special."

My problem, she went on, was not a lack of ability, but of ambition, which came from my lack of humility. Smugness kept me from going on to greater things. I should think bigger. Precision was important, so was accuracy. There should be a conclusion, without vagueness, a sense of completion. To anyone who had been paying attention, what I had accomplished so far was impressive, but to anyone who had not, I was not impossible to ignore. Did I understand what she was saying? Her advice was to imagine myself three to five years from now, then multiply that by ten. That would be who I would become. "I'm not saying you need to be one of those people who plan out their every move. That's a waste of time and talent, in my opinion, since things don't turn out the way we expect them to. But imagination is how we tap the energy of the world. I'm not talking about what writers like Yvonne or your father do, which doesn't strike me as imaginative. Businesspeople like you and me are the true artists of the world."

It was the same pitch, irresistible to receive in person. The song that brought Lincoln and Rafael each to their own ends: for Lincoln, a new life on a boat, perhaps not quite what he hoped; for Rafael, disaster. None of it sounded likely nor interesting to me. It was her ambition, not mine. But it was what happened.

We picked one and found ourselves in a small gallery. It was cluttered, not just with art, but ordinary furniture, clothing tossed over chairs, mugs, and rugs. She chatted up the only person there, who happened to be the curator. The works on the walls seemed to be depictions of the room they occupied. They were of the same medium as Ms. Hu's paintings, pure black ink strokes and gray washes on paper, but of a very different, rather violent style. The subject matter could be said to be antithetical: the cluttered insides of a modern-day apartment, rendered in exaggerated depth perspective.

The room could be Lena's. Or, to be precise, Rafael's, or Margaret's. If she hung it in that apartment, it would be a Russian doll, one inside (the painting) the other (the actual).

On impulse she bought it. I did not know many people who purchased art. Traditional Chinese paintings, mostly Ms. Hu's, hung in my parent's home, but all of those were gifts from the artist, while a work by a stranger had always seemed to me an extravagance. She said art was what spoke to her in the moment; otherwise, it was not worth buying. If she did move out, as now seemed likely, and put that painting up in her new home, wherever it would be, it would act as a window onto her former life, to her past, which did not seem like her at all.

{18}

YVONNE FINALLY AGREED TO REPLACE MY FATHER as head of the Society. We drafted a short Q&A introducing her to the Society's members, full of the usual remarks, but I wanted from her a more adventurous contribution. In consideration of Ms. Hu's ambition to revive the Society literary journal, would she be interested in providing a preview of her next novel? This elicited a burst of laughter. She was not against the idea of the journal, although she felt the production challenges were beyond our current resources. It was just that there would be no next novel. Of course it was the same every time she finished a book, and maybe this mood too would pass, but she had the feeling this time it would not; the total lack of any reception or sales had left her enervated, and the thought of doing it again was discouragement enough. This had no bearing on the Society; she was a real estate agent more than she had ever been a writer, but literature would always be there, whether she liked it or not.

She was old enough to come to peace with this fact, an acquiescence which came with Ms. Hu's offer. Besides, the Society would not be around much longer. It would die out when

Ms. Hu left this world, so we should make the most of it while we could. That was something to consider if I managed to put out an issue of this journal: at the rate we could produce them, how many more would there be? One? Two? If we all somehow stayed on, it might make sense, after the inevitable event, to prepare for future newsletters to be published in English. What other way would the Society begin its long put-off accommodation to its adopted home? As she had actually discussed with Ms. Hu, the current path we were on led straight to the grave, so Yvonne should only serve as a transitional figurehead. Of course, I had no obligation to hang around. From what she saw, I was only doing this to appease my father. I had to admit an English-language Society held no interest for me. Whom would I solicit for work?

As for the translation of my father's book, it never arrived, but some time later, after his passing, I did receive a letter about it. The sender identified herself as my sister's former colleague. She was sorry for not being more diligent; it seemed the world conspired to distract us from our labors of love. If nothing else, she had been compelled to return to the project with greater ardor, but this time, as she reopened the book my sister had given her, a folded sheet of thin Chinese writing paper slipped from between its pages. Script in fine red ink filled its boxes. She could not help thinking the handwriting belonged to my father, since my sister had told her the story of how he had personally handed her the book the last time she saw him.

Her first question, then, was if I could verify the handwriting on the page. For reference, the original was enclosed; she had made a copy for herself.

Her other question was something perhaps I could not answer, but she thought she would ask anyway. If the writing on the paper was my father's, then was the text there meant to be a supplement or revision to the published edition? If I read it, I would understand her reasons for asking, since it was a curious fragment that fit the book as one of many possible endings. That it had come with her copy, even if it had been placed there by accident, struck her as auspicious. Should she endeavor to translate it too and make it part of her manuscript? Since my father had appointed me to review her translation, she would honor any decision I came to.

I read the fragment, which I have included here. It was in many ways familiar to me, even though I had never read it before. I wrote back saying she could safely exclude it, since I believed my father would have wanted her translation to reflect only the published version. After I received no reply, I inquired with my sister, who said she had lost touch with her friend. I assumed the project to be abandoned, which was not unusual. As a teacher of mine once said, it was always easier to start these kinds of things than to finish them.

He walked along C Street, down a mild grade. It was several degrees colder in the range than in the valley. The town's most noticeable features, its roofed plank sidewalks, were still coated in ice and were at any rate impractical for shuttling tourist traffic, given how rickety and seemingly in violation of modern building codes they were. If someone were to slip, they would have to get up on their own power and continue limping along, since there did not seem to be anyone around to help. Once it seemed the

Thinking back, it's possible my ignored reply was an evasion. Who knew what my father would have really wanted, but I did believe inserting an alternative ending to his book, one based wholly on conjecture, would have been the wrong thing to do. It presented unnecessary complications to what should have been the most lucid of narratives, but perhaps too, I had acted out of self-interest, for by liberating the fragment from any previous association, I had freed its use for my own purposes.

The entire exchange remained forgotten until I began work on this account. In fact I was well into a first draft, comparing my father's and Yvonne's renditions of the same scene, when main part of town was thinning, he hung a U-turn and went back up the slope, on the other side of the street. This was the eastern side, still in shadow. The circuit, no more than a few blocks, took longer than it looked, because of the precarious ice, and the cold was bitter and hard to take. Dirty snow piled up in blind alleys. For relief from the weather, he dropped into the few open shops that sat huddled and waiting for the rare visitor.

Keeping his head down against the wind, he tried a door, an old one of painted wood, with a small window at eye level. Although the sign in its window had been flipped to OPEN, the knob would not turn. He looked up. Through the glass the restaurant was empty. He walked to the end of the building and squeezed into a crack between it and the neighboring structure, emerging from the crevice to the delivery entrances on the other side. Not a soul around, but there were more signs of recent activity here than on the main street, in the form of shreds of red paper in the snow. At the

I remembered the existence of yet another. It was not immediately clear what I should do with it, although I dimly perceived a place for its reappropriation. After a life of drifting, from one page to another and one book to another book, that piece, if it were a kind of ending, might now be reunited with all that preceded it.

Perhaps, I thought, it might work here?

same time, the placement of the town in desolate wilderness was far more apparent from this side, as the sky opened and winds whipped up from the canyons below, along the cliff to which the city clung. Shards of windblown ice overhead skidded from eave to eave.

The back door of the restaurant was unlocked. It was a relief to be embraced by the warmth and the dark. The missing people all sounded as if they were in there, the source of the low hum of conversation and the unmistakable click of mahjong tiles. His vision adjusted to the shadows and moved toward the light, into the kitchen, where the stove had been shut off, no smells of cooking, just that of old wood. The shades had been left up. The mahjong clicks accelerated into a raucous clatter as tiles were pushed to the center of the table.

A person was at the counter, in red cheongsam, reading a book. This was the scene he had glimpsed from the other side of the glass. At the time she had not been in it. Now she looked up. The book's

---

[20] As if to break it out from its narrative frame and give it life, my father taped this unattributed handwritten fragment to the manuscript page. Unlike the other interwoven pieces, but like the main trunk of the book, it is rendered by hand, with the same penmanship, only in lurid red instead of black ink. One might imagine he set this section down at an alternate moment from the composition of the bulk, deciding at a later date to bring it into the fold, and from the yellowed quality of the paper and faded script, there is reason to believe it was written much earlier. Was it a cutting from something composed in his youth, reintegrated into a different final draft, all these years later? It is not clear who the protagonist is. Its immediate context suggests it is the narrator who has been with us all this time, but if this is a fragment from an older work, it might have originally been another character altogether, or if a memoir or essay, none other than the author himself.

Acknowledgments

I am grateful to Stephen Beachy, Sarah Blackman, Joanna Ruocco, and the FC2 editorial board for their role in shaping this manuscript; Steve Barbaro, for the *vision*; and Akin Akinwumi, Susan Daitch, and Karen Tei Yamashita, for their feedback and encouragement. I would also like to acknowledge the great work of the team at the University of Alabama Press, including Dan Waterman, Kristen Hop, Jon Berry, Matthew Revert, Steve Halle, Lily Davenport, Greta Terfruchte, Samantha Huff-Robertson, and Nick Shahan, for making the manifestation of this book a reality, and Kelly Krumie, Vincent James, and the editorial team at *Denver Quarterly*, whose publication of a story of mine became its genesis.